## THE WARREN OMISSIONS

*"What can be more fascinating than a super high concept novel that reopens the conspiracy behind the JFK assassination while the threat of a global world war rests in the balance? With his new novel, The Warren Omissions, former journalist turned bestselling author R.J. Patterson proves he just might be the next worthy successor to Vince Flynn."*

**- Vincent Zandri**
**bestselling author of THE REMAINS**

*"R.J. Patterson does a fantastic job at keeping you engaged and interested. I look forward to more from this talented author."*

**- Aaron Patterson**
**bestselling author of SWEET DREAMS**

## CROSS HAIRS

*"Small town life in southern Idaho might seem quaint and idyllic to some. But when local newspaper reporter Cal Murphy begins to uncover a series of strange deaths that are linked to a sticky spider web of deception, the lid on the peaceful town is blown wide open. Told with all the energy and bravado of an old pro, first-timer R.J. Patterson hits one out of the park his first time at bat with Cross Hairs. It's that good."*

**- Vincent Zandri**
**NY Times bestselling author of THE REMAINS**

*"You can tell R.J. knows what it's like to live in the newspaper world, but with Cross Hairs, he's proven that he also can write one heck of a murder mystery."*

**- Josh Katzowitz**
**NFL writer for CBSSports.com**
**& author of Sid Gillman: Father of the Passing Game**

### CROSS THE LINE

*"This book kept me on the edge of my seat the whole time. I didn't really want to put it down. R.J. Patterson has hooked me. I'll be back for more."*

**- Bob Behler**
**3-time Idaho broadcaster of the year**
**and play-by-play voice for Boise State football**

### DEAD IN THE WATER

*"In Dead in the Water, R.J. Patterson accurately captures the action-packed saga of a what could be a real-life college football scandal. The sordid details will leave readers flipping through the pages as fast as a hurry-up offense."*

**- Mark Schlabach, ESPN college sports columnist and**
**co-author of Called to Coach and Heisman:**
**The Man Behind the Trophy**

# THE COOPER AFFAIR

### *A JAMES FLYNN THRILLER*
*Book 3*

## R.J. PATTERSON

THE COOPER AFFAIR
© Copyright 2015 R.J. Patterson

First Print Edition 2016
Second Print Edition 2017


Cover Design by Dan Pitts


Published in the United States of America
Green E-Books
Boise, Idaho 83714

*To my dad,*
*for always stirring my imagination with history and science*

*Conspiracy theorists of the world, believers in the hidden hands of the Rothschilds and the Masons and the Illuminati, we skeptics owe you an apology. You were right. The players may be a little different, but your basic premise is correct: The world is a rigged game.*

*— Auliq Ice*

# THE COOPER AFFAIR

# CHAPTER 1

CARLTON GORDON had not considered making the drunk, homeless man everyone called Doc an accomplice in his lifelong dream. Gordon would thrust the unsuspecting soul—usually found a couple of blocks away from his girl-friend Felicia's apartment on the corner of 22nd and Capp Street—into a world of scrutiny he most certainly wouldn't welcome. But he could live with the guilt.

He watched as Doc slowly raised the cigarette to his lips and took a long drag, releasing the smoke slowly and looking skyward. Doc's steady gaze on a plane soaring overhead gave off the impression that he seemed interested in it.

"I always wonder where they're going, too," Gordon said as he glanced at his watch.

Doc took another drag and shook his head. "I never think about where they're goin'," he said as the smoke rushed out of his mouth and swirled upward. "I always wonder why anyone on board ever left."

Gordon looked at his watch again, the Rolex sparkling from the late afternoon sun. "Perhaps they have business elsewhere."

Doc shook his head again. "Well, Mr. Money Bags, I'm of the opinion that nobody has any business gettin' on an airplane unless they have a death wish."

Gordon smiled at the nickname Doc had bestowed upon him several months ago, but he couldn't wait on the old man any longer. Gordon snatched the cigarette from Doc's hands just as he was about to take his final drag. He snuffed it out against the wall behind Doc.

"Hey! What'd ya do that for?" Doc protested. "That Raleigh still had one more good drag left."

"Sorry, Doc. I've gotta catch a plane."

\*\*\*

TWO HOURS LATER, Gordon settled into the plane, though it was his first time flying in such a unique position. He didn't hold a ticket, though he almost wished he had one as a memento; anything with the date November 24 on it would suffice. But he didn't—and if truth be told, it was hardly *that* important to him. What he was about to *do* was something he'd dreamed about for much of his adult life ever since he read about the infamous D.B. Cooper, though he was well versed enough with the case to know that Dan Cooper was the infamous hijacker's nom de guerre, not D.B. The initials were the result of a simple miscommunication during transcription of the criminal mastermind's name used to board Northwest Orient Airlines Flight 305 from Portland to Seattle more than 40 years ago. Gordon jammed his earplugs in and closed his eyes while a smile swept across his face.

Prone and stiff, Gordon shifted as the plane's engines roared. This wasn't the first time he'd been on his back in a jet. He never traveled to Europe without purchasing a first class ticket, usually two—the second designated for his girlfriend of the week. Women, like most things, never held Gordon's interest for long. D.B. Cooper, however, served as the rare exception.

Gordon's fingertips tingled as the plane rumbled along, gaining speed with each passing moment. After what felt like minutes but was surely only seconds, the nose of the jet tilted skyward and the plane lifted off the ground. He glanced at his watch and marked the time. In a hundred minutes, he would prepare to exit the plane. One minute after that, he'd leap to safety before anyone could figure out what was happening. That is, if his calculations were correct—and he knew they were. He'd spent the better part of a decade devising a scheme to emulate his criminal hero. It felt old hat to him, like he'd done this a hundred times before. And he had—in his mind. Every detail crafted with exquisite precision. That is, every detail except Doc.

Employing the old man's lungs was an afterthought, the one thing he'd forgotten to plan for. He couldn't believe he could be so careless, though this wasn't crucial to his crime—just a touch of craftsmanship. That's how he felt in his mind anyway. If he wanted to pay homage to his hero, Gordon needed to add style, something that proved he was more than an average criminal. He prided himself on being a thinking man, one whose intelligence always made him the smartest man in the room. After he pulled off this stunt, he'd be considered the second man who outsmarted the FBI after jumping out of a plane with stacks of cash, all while paying tribute to the first.

If Gordon were greedy, he could make off with far more. The shipment from the U.S. Treasury in San Francisco to Seattle during the burgeoning holiday season appeared to be close to eight million, give or take a few hundred thousand. If he weren't shoehorned into the aft cargo hold, he might be able to make a more accurate estimate. As a manager for Seattle's biggest downtown branch for Bank of Olympia, he'd seen pallets of money during visits to the U.S. Treasury branch in San Francisco and the Bureau of Engraving and Printing in Fort Worth, Texas. He always asked how much was on the pallet until he started to judge for himself and would bet lunch on the fact that he could guess within ten thousand dollars. He won three lunches off his liaison in Fort Worth before the man started refusing to play Gordon's game.

But there could've been twenty or thirty million in the cargo hold of this jet and it wouldn't have mattered to Gordon. This wasn't about the money. He only cared about experiencing what D.B. Cooper experienced when he disappeared over southeastern Washington with twenty-two pounds of twenty-dollar bills. When it came to hundred-dollar bills, Gordon's weight was the same for a million dollars as it was for Cooper's two hundred thousand.

Money meant nothing to him, not now anyway. Years ago, it was his life pursuit. He amassed his fortune first as a small business owner serving the niche equestrian market, then as a day trader. But the boredom of being his own boss grated on him until he decided to merge his expertise of both running a business and understanding the financial market. The result was his current position with his bank. Yet the folded-up medical report in his pocket served as a constant reminder that money didn't matter now. He only had a few months to live, according to his doctor. And he wasn't going to exit the world without emulating his favorite villain.

It wasn't a perfect replication of Cooper's infamous 1971 crime; that was something Gordon deemed impossible after terrorists' actions on 9/11 resulted in the closure of every loophole. But his way would be close enough. And anyone paying attention would understand what he was doing.

Gordon checked his watch. Seventy-five minutes to go. He sighed and wondered if he could wait that long, though he knew he must, especially if he was going to truly honor his hero.

***

GORDON FELT A CHILL, though it was nothing close to the freezing air he'd experience when he jumped out of the plane in three minutes. He fished the plastic bag out of his pocket that contained the eight Raleigh cigarettes Doc had smoked. He wedged it beneath one of the cargo containers so it wouldn't be lost in the violent windstorm that would strike the aft cargo the moment he blew the doors open.

He checked his watch again and noted the time. He didn't have a moment to spare. Slithering through the cargo hold toward the center of the plane, Gordon got onto his knees and hid behind a container. He pushed a button on the small device in his hand, blowing open the door.

On his hands and knees, he scurried toward the door. Before he left, Gordon glanced once more at the plastic bag lodged beneath a container. It was his care package for the feds once they inevitably tore the plane apart looking for clues. He knew they wouldn't find anything that would lead to him, but they would find something that pointed to someone who admired D.B. Cooper. It'd be a big middle finger at the Bureau. The one skyjacking case that had never been solved—and never would be solved as long as they continued to ignore all credible evidence that a guy named Kenny Christensen was likely behind it all—was about to be repeated.

But Gordon didn't care who they chased or who they ignored. A new generation of Americans was about to have a fresh appreciation for D.B. Cooper's ability to pull off the perfect crime—along with a new criminal to admire. It was a byproduct of his crime that he was prepared for, one that he expected. And like Cooper, Gordon wanted to avoid getting caught. Just one misstep and he'd be headed for federal prison—but he had a backup plan for that, too.

Gordon edged closer to the door. He secured his gear before placing both hands on the sides of the opening and pulling himself forward. He went head over heels into the crisp Washington air. He'd leapt from this height before and knew what it'd feel like, though he was convinced it was something nobody could ever truly prepare for. The blast of cold air and the sensation of hurtling toward the ground always felt new even though it wasn't.

Beneath Gordon, the Nisqually National Wildlife Refuge appeared serene, motionless. It looked like a picture, a perfect moment drawn and frozen for him to enjoy. But it was so much more. To Gordon, it was a way out, the pathway to escape and commit the perfect crime—a crime he planned to repeat in a few days time.

For now, he chose to enjoy the view as the wind whipped against him with only a few twinkling stars to keep him company as he descended through the dusky sky.

*So this is what it feels like to be D.B. Cooper.*

# CHAPTER 2

JAMES FLYNN TOOK A SHARP RIGHT off state highway 503 and followed the signs toward the Ariel General Store & Tavern. Only a two-lane stretch of road and a meandering swath of water known as Lake Merwin parted the thick woods coating the area just an hour northeast of Portland. In his two previous trips to the area, Flynn wondered the same thing as he was at the moment—how anyone could safely land in these woods, much less do so in the dark? Though he was about to walk into a party celebrating the man who'd duped the FBI and gotten away with the perfect crime, he doubted anyone could survive such an unforgiving part of the country regardless of the time of day.

Flynn slowed his car to a crawl, creeping past the cars and trucks lining the two-lane road toward the tavern. Flynn chuckled again at the irony dripping from Ariel the moment he entered the unincorporated area. A handmade speed limit sign warned drivers: "Show some respect" sat atop a large "25," while the phrase "It's the law" rested below it. An odd statement for a town whose claim to fame was celebrating a man who broke the law in the grandest way possible.

After finding a spot along the road to park, Flynn hiked up a hill toward the tavern. Before he set foot inside, a man dressed as D.B. Cooper greeted him on the steps.

"The perfect crime must be celebrated with the perfect

beer," the man said. He thrust a sampler cup into Flynn's hand. "Enjoy."

The words "Rainier Beer" were emblazoned on the side. Flynn took one sip and nearly spit it out. It tasted like an Old Milwaukee knockoff, though he wondered why anyone would want to produce such a watered-down brew, especially no more than an hour away from one of the biggest craft beer hubs in the country.

Inside, Flynn saw a handful of other men dressed as Cooper. If they'd been in Vegas, they would've been Elvis impersonators; of that much Flynn was sure. Some of the men appeared as corporate shills like the Rainier Beer man, but most were there to win a contest and $200. If they had the money, Flynn figured the prize would have been set at $200,000 as just another tip of the cap to the man everyone there revered.

"What can I do ya for?" barked the bartender, sliding a napkin toward Flynn as he found a seat at the bar.

"Give me Washington's finest," Flynn said.

A few moments later, the man returned with a frosty mug filled with an amber-colored beer.

"This place hasn't changed much," Flynn said.

The bartender nodded and stuck out his hand. "Aaron Matthews," the man said. "And you are?"

"James Flynn. I'm with *The National* magazine," he said, holding fast to the man's grip.

"Welcome to Ariel—and D.B. Cooper Days," Matthews said. "And, yes, it hasn't changed. Yet most days, it's nothing more than a bunch of old loggers pining about the way it used to be—no pun intended."

Flynn snickered. "That much fun, huh?"

"Like a barrel of monkeys."

Flynn nursed his beer, while he looked around the room and hoped to find enough interesting people to interview for the article his editor, Theresa Thompson from *The National* magazine, had assigned him. He saw a fertile field of characters to talk to, most of whom he hoped were quite soused by this point in the night to provide a little extra color to his story. As he wandered around and spoke with different patrons, no one seemed truly interested in exploring the truth. It was more like a festival to share conspiracy theories and consume the trendiest Portland or Seattle swill.

As the day transitioned into night, Flynn received more and more farfetched theories. Some tavern patrons claimed it was an inside job by an FBI agent. Others claimed an airline executive orchestrated the heist. The more cynical of the crowd said the man had died, as they refused to believe there was any way he could've escaped the forest.

Then at 10 p.m., the tavern fell silent.

On the screen, a newscaster shared the news of how a man leapt out of a plane with a million dollars during a flight from San Francisco to Seattle. According to the report, all passengers were accounted for, leaving officials scratching their heads as to how this man could've pulled off such a stunt.

The timing of the heist wasn't lost on anyone in the tavern.

After a moment of awkward silence, one bearded man hoisted his mug in the air and yelled, "D.B. Cooper strikes again!"

"Here! Here!" said another man.

What followed next were a series of guffaws and the

clinking of glasses—along with new theories hatched on the spot.

Maybe it was D.B. Cooper's son? Could D.B. Cooper replicate his crime at 85 years of age? A copycat crime seemed to be the prevailing theory circulating around the room, but that could all change in a matter of seconds. A newscaster could debunk it all with a report centered around an interview from the FBI agent on the case. But that didn't happen.

Nothing.

The news anchor dangled the information—and the tavern in Ariel ran with it, creating fascinating theory after fascinating theory. Flynn couldn't believe any of them. But he couldn't ignore them either.

He needed a story. The whole country would be onto this before midnight.

Flynn had to find a compelling angle—and fast.

# CHAPTER 3

HAROLD COLEMAN WOULD'VE LEAPT off his recliner if he were able. Instead, he just threw his cane toward the television and let out a string of profanities. The older he became, the more he cursed—but even this was more than usual for him. It drew the concern of his wife, Betty.

She shuffled into the room, wiping her hands on her apron. "What is it, Harold? Why are you so upset?"

"Somebody's trying to copy D.B. Cooper's crime," he said, waving his hand dismissively at the television.

"I see," she said, rolling her eyes and sighing. Before she could say another word, the newscaster uttered a sentence that made her husband go from upset to livid.

The man with a chiseled jaw and slick dark hair delivered his line with what sounded like a mocking tone to Harold: "Tonight's heist comes on the anniversary of D.B. Cooper's infamous skyjacking, a crime that former FBI investigator Harold Coleman and his team failed to solve and remains unsolved to this day."

Coleman stood up and shook his fist at the television before stumbling toward his cane. He slowly knelt down to pick it up. When he stood upright, he used his cane like a baseball bat to smack the screen. It wasn't hard enough to cause any damage, something his wife made sure of by hustling toward him and putting her arms around him.

"It's okay, Harold," she said. "They're not blaming you. It's just a news story. No one would've caught him."

Coleman struggled to free himself from his wife's grip before he lumbered back toward his chair and sat down. He snatched the remote from the table next to him and turned off the television.

"The bastard's dead. Case closed," he snarled. "Why does every blood-sucking journalist need a body to prove what we already know? If Cooper wasn't a tasty snack for a bear, his body was surely devoured by some animal."

"Calm down, dear," Betty said. "You know how everyone just loves a good conspiracy."

"Not me. I hate 'em, especially any time they're related to Cooper."

"I know—but you've got to let the newscasters have their fun, okay? There are only so many fundraisers for environmental conservation to fill an evening newscast in Portland."

Coleman laughed, snickering at his wife's dry wit. Besides, she was right. This was a juicy story based on the history of Cooper and his legendary leap from that plane more than forty years ago.

He leaned back in his chair and closed his eyes, reliving each moment like it was yesterday. Nobody at the time believed Cooper could've survived the jump into that terrain under those conditions. And the ones who believed it today? Coleman wrote them off as fame whores. Like anything in this day and age, if someone presented a theory contrary to popular opinion, it was sure to find the light of day. It's how some people built their followings.

Coleman didn't care. He knew the truth. Cooper had never been found. And the long list of suspects—Floyd McCoy, Gary Samdel, Joseph H. Johnston, John Hoskin, Louis Macaluso, James Henry Zimmerman, William Warwick—proved to be one dead end after another. If Cooper had survived, Coleman knew he would've found him. The only logical explanation was that he wasn't alive, the thief and his money consumed by nature's fiercest and finest. It wasn't a cruel twist of fate, but an act of justice—and mercy. If Coleman had ever laid hands on Cooper, it wouldn't have been pretty.

But what Coleman just witnessed on the news stirred something in him—a second chance. He was old, but he still had his wits.

He was going to help the feds catch this man and bring him to justice—dead or alive.

# CHAPTER 4

GORDON PULLED HIS HOOD SNUG and kept his head down as he exited the train and walked toward his condominium. Each time he passed a person on the street, he wondered if they could see the money hanging from pockets he'd created in his coat. Instinctively, he wanted to glance up at the street cameras, but he fought the urge, knowing the danger just one full facial look at the camera would cause him.

*Just breathe. You're almost home.*

Instead of entering his high-rise condo the normal way, Gordon slipped through the alleyway and prepared to enter through a back exit. The door was supposed to be open, cracked just enough for him to wedge his fingers into it and open it, but not enough that anyone would realize it was open. In preparation for the heist, he put a camera on the door to monitor how often it was used. In three weeks of tapes, he saw two people use the door, both on Friday nights. It was Tuesday and he assumed he'd be in the clear.

*Just a small sliver of wood should do the trick.*

At least, that's what he thought when he hatched his plan. But as he rounded the corner, his eyes fell immediately to the spot he'd left the piece of wood.

It was gone.

Shallow breathing. Walking in circles.

*Take a deep breath. All is not lost. Calm down.*

If he went into the lobby, the camera could capture him along with the fingerprint identification key necessary to access the elevator and the stairwell lock. He couldn't avoid both, though even evading one proved challenging. Were he to become a suspect, he needed his alibi to remain airtight. There could be no wiggle room for the prosecutor to establish his whereabouts as anywhere but where he said they were. There could be no room for the jury's suspicion.

His options were limited. He could walk around downtown for hours until the second part of his plan fell into place, though he still risked getting captured by a surveillance camera somewhere. If he remained where he was, he still faced the problem of being in public long enough for someone to identify him.

Neither of those options worked for Gordon. He needed to get into his apartment and out of sight without anyone noticing him.

*Think, Gordon. Think.*

His perfectly crafted plan suddenly seemed riddled with holes. He slumped against the wall in the alleyway and thought about another possible way. His criteria included not getting identified in his building on the security camera or with the fingerprint identification log. The more he pondered his options, the less hopeful he became.

Until now, his execution of the plan remained flawless. Now it was a dumpster fire—at least it felt that way.

Then an idea sparked in his mind.

He got up and walked several blocks toward a district that was known for its dive bars and meth junkies. With his sunglasses on and his hood cropped tightly around his face, Gordon sauntered up and down a block, surveying his potential recruits. After a few minutes, he made his choice.

Gordon knelt down next to a young man with a scraggly beard. He wore an army green jacket and a pair of boots with gaping holes in the toes. Leaning against the wall with his feet extended outward, his head drooped.

Gordon took a firm grip on the man's bicep and shook him.

"Hey, man! What are you doing?" the man asked.

In an effort to disguise his identity, Gordon conjured up a guttural voice. "What's your name, kid?"

"Kid? Who you callin' 'kid'?"

Gordon sighed and shook his head. "Would you prefer I call you a 'Meth Head Adult'?"

The man withdrew. "Leave me alone, dude. You're interrupting my sleep."

"How would you like to make an easy hundred bucks?"

The man sat up. "I'm listening."

Gordon gave the man instructions and then slapped a hundred dollar bill into his hand, a bill he'd fished out from his wallet instead of his jacket to make sure they couldn't trace the money back to him—if the authorities would even bother to look for him.

Gordon followed the man at a safe distance back toward his condominium. In a matter of minutes, the junkie reached the condominium. And just as directed, he wandered inside and pulled the fire alarm before rushing outside.

Within a few minutes, more than a hundred people spilled out of the condo and onto the sidewalk, most of whom Gordon didn't recognize. Once everyone realized it was a false alarm and began re-entering the building, Gordon slipped in with the mass of people. No need to use his fingerprint identification now.

He slipped onto a crowded elevator, his best option for remaining forgettable. The woman with the large bust and skimpy dress attracted the most attention. He kept his head down and smiled at his good fortune. By the stop on the twenty-first floor, everyone exited. He was in the clear.

Almost.

"Carlton? Is that you?" a woman cried out from down the hall of the twenty-first floor, her heels clicking on the marble as she waddled toward the elevator.

*Keep your head down. She can't see your face.*

Gordon punched the button for the thirtieth floor several times.

*Come on, come on.*

The doors began to close as the click-clack of Mrs. Danaman's shoes approached with urgency.

He hadn't seen her in over two months—and he hadn't called her back since then either. He'd run into her at a local bar. She was tipsy. He was drunk. It was a disaster, a mistake he chose to forget. He couldn't let her ruin his plan.

Gordon peered beneath his hood at Mrs. Danaman—or, as she was more affectionately known in social circles, "Cookie"—as she reached to push the elevator button to keep it open. But as she did, the doors clinked shut and the elevator hummed, carrying him upward.

He sighed in relief as he proceeded to push several buttons for floors above and below his. Gordon needed to confuse the socialite just in case she recognized him and was watching the floor numbers on the display to confirm her suspicions.

The elevator dinged on his floor and he rushed out toward his condo door. He checked both directions of the hall. Nothing. He shoved his key into the lock and went inside.

*Disaster averted.*

He tumbled into his favorite recliner and turned on the news in time to watch a segment about his exploits. No footage yet but they were already calling him the D.B. Cooper Copycat. It wasn't original, but he could live with it.

He flung his jacket onto the couch and stared at the stacks of hundred dollar bills.

*I did it.*

He smiled, satisfied that he managed to pull off the heist.

But he was just getting started.

He was going to do it again.

# CHAPTER 5

JAMES FLYNN LEANED ON HIS CIA contacts when he wanted to find out what was going on during a criminal investigation. But since this case was strictly domestic, he needed to look elsewhere, specifically in the direction of the FBI. It was only a matter of time before his editor called him demanding an update on the story—and he was going to have as many answers as possible for her.

He looked at his watch and took a swig of coffee.

*Five minutes past seven on a Monday morning. I'm sure she's up by now.*

Flynn hesitated before knocking on the door.

A few shoeless footsteps on hardwood floor, then a feminine yet firm voice. "Yes?"

"It's James Flynn," he said. "I come bearing caffeine."

The light sneaking through the eyehole vanished and reappeared again as the deadbolt lock clicked.

"Grande soy latte, no whip cream?" the dark-haired woman at the door asked after she pulled it open.

Flynn nodded and put the drink in her hand. "I never forget a coffee order."

She rolled her eyes and waved him inside. "I didn't think I'd see you so soon again. What brings you to Seattle?"

"Do you need to ask?"

A faint smile crept across the woman's lips. "I always

ask. It's what I do."

Flynn shook his head. Jennifer Banks, FBI agent extraordinaire—at least, that's how he perceived her. He'd remained enamored with her since their last adventure across the country to stop a potential bio terror threat and save the Capitol building from becoming a permanent quarantine zone. He couldn't believe his good fortune to get to work with her again so soon—that is, if she'd let him. And he had a feeling she would.

"Well, I'm hoping that you're working on the Cooper Copycat case," he said. "Am I in luck?"

She smiled. "Indeed you are—but I have a feeling you already knew I was." She held up her coffee cup. "You think this little gift is going to get you in on the action?"

"I'm very familiar with the original case."

"As are most FBI agents and conspiracy theorists. Not sure I can see the value in letting you in on this one. My partner, Chase Jones, is very capable."

"I'm not trying to replace him. But perhaps you don't understand—this is the case I've obsessed about since I started working at *The National*. I know every piece of trivia there is to know about D.B. Cooper."

"Every piece?"

"Try me."

"What kind of plane did he jump out of?"

Flynn sighed. "Seriously? I thought you were going to ask me some tough questions."

Banks took a sip of her latte. "What kind of cigarettes did Cooper smoke?"

"Raleighs." He shook his head. "This is child's play. Can you please ask me something worthy of my D.B.

Cooper obsession?"

"What color shoes was he wearing?"

"Brown."

"How did he cut his sideburns?"

"Low ear level."

She cracked a faint smile. "His voice?"

"Low, but no real discernible accent, though some FBI profiles suggested he was from the Midwest."

She shrugged. "Not bad, but you haven't proven that you'd be helpful on this case."

"You know my background with the CIA. It couldn't hurt to have me around, could it?"

She shook her head. "You're incorrigible. I'll come up with something." She stood up. "Let's go."

"You won't be sorry."

She stopped and stared at him. "Just promise me one thing."

"What's that?"

"Don't publish anything about this case without my permission. Is that understood?"

Flynn nodded. Behind his back he crossed his fingers. It was an old habit, but he didn't want to hamstring why he was really there—to find out the identity of Cooper's copycat and write about it. His word was only good when it suited his agenda; otherwise, all bets were off. He couldn't get at the truth if he made some sophomoric promise to remain tightlipped. And Banks should've known better, at least that's how he justified it to himself.

***

AT THE SEATTLE FIELD OFFICE, Flynn received an

access badge. He didn't know what Banks had told her supervisor, but he didn't want to know either. Whatever it was, she likely lied to get him in the door—and for that, he was grateful. He needed to peek under the covers and see if there was anything else that warranted being told to the general public. The more information the FBI withheld, the less chance they had of capturing him.

Flynn took the position that crowdsourcing was the best way to catch a criminal on the run. In the digital age, no one could outrun social media. Someone always wanted to be a hero on the Internet. But Banks didn't share the same sentiment—and neither did the FBI.

In the initial briefing, Flynn took notes on what information had already been regurgitated to the public: the who, what, when, where, and how of the crime. But the *who* was nothing more than a moniker bestowed upon the copycat by the FBI. And the *why*? The FBI seemed clueless.

To Flynn, this wasn't a crime that needed to be solved by rehashing every detail. It was a crime that could only be solved by determining why it was committed. And it was very evident to him that the criminal was obsessed with D.B. Cooper, which was to Flynn's advantage.

Since joining *The National*, Flynn had been assigned to write about Cooper's skyjacking at least three times. It had been a source of constant conversation whenever he returned to the office. And he estimated that at least twenty percent of the emails requesting he look into a particular conspiracy asked about D.B. Cooper. It ran neck-and-neck with emails asking why so many people affiliated with the Clinton administration died. He preferred not to touch the latter, lest he end up just like all the people who supposedly crossed the Clintons in one way or another. But the former? He wanted to get to the bottom of the Cooper hijacking more than his readers did—of that much he was confident.

Flynn found an office and pounded out a short piece on the investigation.

## D.B. Cooper Revisited?

FBI officials remain baffled as to how a D.B. Cooper copycat managed to pull off a heist of a similar nature Saturday night.

According to officials, the man who leapt out of a commercial jet Saturday over the Seattle metro area absconded with $1 million, leaving behind more than $5 million in the plane on its way to Seattle area banks. With the holiday season fast approaching, FAA officials will be tightening security to squelch any opportunity of such a heist happening again.

While FBI officials declined to go on record, the identity of the criminal remains a mystery. In cursory investigations, no footage of the criminal has surfaced, while officials continue to determine a motive for the crime.

Despite the fact that the crime wasn't an exact duplication of the 1971 skyjacking that remains unsolved, the similarities were evident. The amount of money involved may seem like a difference since D.B.

Cooper only made off with $200,000, but the money was given to him in $20 bills. The $1 million taken from the San Francisco to Seattle flight was equivalent to the weight of the money stolen in the original heist. And the fact that the thief jumped near Seattle wasn't lost on investigators, nor was the date.

So far, officials have remained mum about who might be behind it, though they are determined to flush him out and apprehend him—no matter what it takes.

Flynn grinned as he hit the send button. It would surely raise Banks' ire, but he figured he could smooth things over and avoid any long-term damage. He still had a job to do, which involved covering the story and gaining plenty of eyeballs on the magazine's webpage. He wasn't sure that he accomplished his main objective for the time being, but it would serve notice that *The National* was on top of the story and would be the go-to website for coverage of the crime.

He got up and wandered down the hall toward Banks' desk. She was in her supervisor's office, undoubtedly discussing the case. He looked around before he peeked inside the manila folder on her desk. He found a report detailing what investigators found in their initial search of the aft cargo hold of Flight #419. A plastic baggie full of Raleigh cigarettes. No hair fibers. No fingerprints. And a newspaper clipping from 1971 about D.B. Cooper.

*And not a single viable suspect.*

To Flynn, it sounded like 1971 all over again.

A loud commotion down the hallway snapped him out of his trance. He turned to look near the fracas and an elderly gentleman was waving his hands wildly and yelling at the security officers trying to turn him around and escort him out of the building.

Flynn was intrigued, as he knew stories like these brought all the crazies out. He wanted to further investigate but his phone buzzed, reminding him of a scheduled radio program appointment. "Beyond Words," with Allister McKinley, was a popular nationally syndicated talk show that aired in every major market—and he'd been asked him to come on the air and talk about the heist. He determined not to say anything more than what he wrote in his online piece for *The National* to avoid further confrontation with Banks. But it was necessary. The public needed to know what was going on if law enforcement officials were ever going to catch Cooper's copycat.

He dialed his phone while the mayhem at the end of the hall continued.

# CHAPTER 6

HAROLD COLEMAN RESISTED the security guard who gripped his bicep while attempting to usher him down the hall. Though he appeared old and frail, Coleman wasn't having any of it. He threw an elbow into the guard's stomach and stood upright.

"Will someone get me the agent in charge of the Cooper copycat case?" he said.

The guard reached out to grab him when Brad Thurston walked up. Thurston put his hand up and shook his head, signaling the guard to leave the man alone.

Coleman snapped his head back over his shoulder and glared at the guard.

"Mr. Coleman, what can I do for you?" Thurston said as he placed a firm hand on Coleman's shoulder.

"You know who I am?" Coleman sneered.

"I think the entire floor knows who you are by now— but I knew who you were the second I saw your face. I've seen that mug of yours on my television screen more times than I care to count during D.B. Cooper documentaries."

Coleman forced a smile. "Good. Then I think you know why I'm here."

"To relive the good ole days?"

Coleman furrowed his brow. "I want to help. And

nobody knows this case better than me. Just bring me on as a special consultant."

Thurston pivoted and gestured with an outstretched arm down the hall. "Let's talk in my office."

Coleman clenched his fists as he shuffled down the hall. He knew exactly where this conversation was headed. Thurston would pat him on the back, thank him for his service, and let him know that they had everything under control. But it'd all be disingenuous, patronizing, and untrue—in that order. If anything, Coleman knew what it was like to start digging for a pebble in a pile of boulders. That's how cases like these started, especially in instances where no DNA was available.

When Coleman started working the original Cooper case, he struggled to determine a serious suspect. Making matters worse were the people who desired to claim credit for the crime as D.B. Cooper became more popular and a part of American folklore. And based on the amount of adulation heaped on Cooper by the public, who wouldn't want to be him? Every jailed criminal who'd even thought about jumping out of an airplane and had visited Portland once in their lives tried to claim credit. Checking out every claim bogged down Coleman's investigation.

He didn't want to see the Bureau make the same mistakes he'd made. Above all, he wanted the bastard caught, if only to deter similar future criminal activities. But if he was honest with himself, there was another reason he wanted to be involved, even it was behind the scenes. He needed closure—and redemption. The Cooper case had always been a nasty mark on his career, one he couldn't rub clean regardless of how hard he tried. Yet this was his chance to whitewash that blemish and find the peace he sought. Sure, he looked old and tired, but he still had his wits—and the Bureau could use every last one of them to catch a brilliantly planned crime.

"Have a seat," Thurston said as he pointed at the chair across from his desk. He closed the door and sat opposite Coleman.

"I'm not interested in hearing some patronizing speech," Coleman said. "I know that my failure to apprehend Cooper—even if I'm confident the scumbag died when he jumped from that airplane—is one of the biggest black eyes in the Bureau's history. I doubt you have much confidence in me either, but let me assure you I have a wealth of knowledge that could be helpful to this case."

Thurston's eyebrows shot upward. "First of all, we're not even sure that this is a Cooper copycat. I know that's what the TV and newspapers are calling this crime, but they'd call a cat a horse if it would earn them more eyeballs on their product. Other than jumping out of an airplane with money, it's not so similar. Secondly, I appreciate your candor, but you're right—your inability to definitively solve the first case is not exactly something I'm interested in reintroducing to this case. It would be a needless distraction for our agents and the Bureau in general."

Coleman leaned forward in his chair. "You *have* to let me help you."

Thurston shook his head. "No, I have to do what I feel is in the Bureau's best interest. I *must* do whatever gives my agents the best shot at solving this crime. Bringing you onboard wouldn't do that, which is something I hope you can understand. It's nothing personal, truly."

Coleman slammed his fist down, partially anger but mostly to help himself stand up. "Your arrogance will be your downfall."

Thurston stood up. "I have more than capable agents. And that's not arrogance—that's a fact." He waved dismissively with the back of his hand. "Now show yourself out."

Coleman turned and shuffled toward the door. He turned and looked over his shoulder, glaring at Thurston. "You're going to come to me begging for help. Mark my word."

Thurston rolled his eyes and gave Coleman another derisive look. He pointed again at the door. "Go."

Coleman swung the door open and entered the hallway, muttering a string of expletives under his breath. Despite his unusual presence, most agents were too busy to notice him—or his smooth swipe of an agent's security access card off her vacant desk.

Coleman almost made it to the elevator when a man grabbed his arm. He withdrew and stared at the man. "Who are you?"

The man offered his hand. "I'm James Flynn, a reporter for *The National*."

Coleman rubbed his forehead and sighed. "Oh, great. Another media member. Are you here to drag my name through the mud again?"

Flynn drew back. "Actually, no. I want to know what similarities you see between the two cases and why you think this may or may not be a Cooper copycat crime?"

Coleman's face lit up. "Walk with me. There are a few things I've never told anyone about the case—but it's about time."

# CHAPTER 7

WHEN GORDON ARRIVED IN HIS OFFICE Tuesday morning, he looked both directions down the hall before closing the door behind him. He wanted to catch all the latest news on his escapade from the previous day—a virtual scrapbook, of sorts. Of course, he needed to search other news as well. If the authorities ever combed through the search history on his computer, he wanted it to be uninteresting.

By his best guess, half the people in Seattle who worked in front of a desktop were reading about the story at the same time. His interest in the case meant nothing. But just in case, he clicked on a few stories about how the city's new $15 minimum wage regulations were hitting the restaurant industry hard as well as another story about the Seahawks' struggles on offense against the Packers in the Monday Night Football game a day ago.

Just another Tuesday in Seattle. It was an endless cycle of complaining, moaning, and blaming. Whether the topic was weather, sports, or local politics, there was always something to gripe about. And Gordon would appear to be armed with all of the hottest topics—though he suspected the only thing anyone would want to talk about was the Cooper

Copycat still on the loose.

He meandered down the hall a few minutes shy of 10:30 to confirm his suspicions. Carl Jaworski's voice could be heard halfway down the hall.

"Does this guy really think he's the second coming of D.B. Cooper?" Jaworski asked his disciples circled near him in the break room. A few of them nodded in approval and mumbled their agreement.

Gordon detested Jaworski's brash attitude, but he couldn't justify firing him since he was such a meticulous worker with an admirable work ethic.

"Times have changed," Gordon said as he slipped past Jaworski and poured himself a cup of coffee. "Aside from the fact that hardly any Boeing 727s with aft stair access are in use today and that you couldn't get a bomb through airport security if your life depended on it, the days of D.B. Cooper have been gone for years. But this guy is definitely the next generation of skyjacking."

"What? Hiding like a coward in the cargo hold and jumping out when it's dark? Yeah. Sounds like a real brazen criminal to me." Jaworski shook his head. "Just another example of the wussification of America. Hell, even our criminals don't have balls any more."

Gordon held up his hand. "Come on, Jaworski. There are ladies present here."

"Yeah. And the ladies here are tougher than our criminals. What do you think that says about the future of this country?"

The other workers backed off slowly as Gordon trudged toward Jaworski. He poked his subordinate in the chest. "You, my friend, have a warped mind. Trying to determine the future of America based off criminal activity? Besides, when did we start detesting the criminals who were doing what we all wished we could do and stick it to Uncle Sam?"

Jaworski pulled back. "No disrespect, but that's messed up. D.B. Cooper isn't some hero—and neither is this guy desperately trying to imitate him, as poor of an imitation as it might be. Both of them are thugs who stole the hard-earned money that you and I forked over through our taxes, not some folk hero to be celebrated."

Gordon sighed. "Times were different back then."

Jaworski waved him off. "Yeah, yeah. I've heard all the spin and seen the documentaries. Times were tough in the area, the logging industry was under attack, and everybody hated the government. Blah, blah, blah. It doesn't change the reality of what he did or what this wannabe did. They're both thieves."

"I guess we'll have to agree to disagree then."

Jaworski chuckled. "And you accuse others of being a wuss? That's the wussiest way out of an argument. It's what people say when they realize their argument is riddled with holes."

Gordon eyed him closely. "Don't you have some loans to approve?"

Jaworski shook his head and walked toward the door. Then he stopped. "I know you don't agree with me, but think about it. Don't try to canonize this guy. I'm sure you wouldn't try to make a hero out of anyone who robbed our bank—no matter what the reason."

Gordon poured himself another cup of coffee and looked at the rest of the workers lingering in the break room.

"Do all of you feel this way?"

A few shrugs, a couple of mumbled responses.

Gordon decided it wasn't worth his breath. He marched back to his office and sat down.

*How can they not cheer for me? I'm doing the same thing Cooper did.*

He shuffled through a few papers and stared at his to-do list for the day. It was lengthy and tedious. He put his hands behind his head and leaned back in his chair. All he could think about was what he had to do next.

A soft tap on his door snapped him back to his senses.

"Come in," he said.

His secretary, Patti Thomas, poked her head in the door. "How are you, sir?"

"It's a Tuesday," he said.

She handed him a stack of documents. "I was wondering if I could get your John Hancock on these files."

"Certainly."

She didn't move.

"Anything else?" he asked.

She furrowed her brow and cocked her head to one side. "Are you feeling better today, sir?"

"Better?"

"Yeah, you didn't seem to be yourself yesterday. Something just seemed off."

He picked up a medicine bottle on his desk. "Maybe it's these new pills I'm taking."

She nodded.

"Why? Did I say something out of line?"

She grimaced. "That's one way of putting it."

He stood up. "Patti, tell me what I did. You know how

I sometimes say things without thinking."

She bobbed her head back and forth. "Well, since you asked." She paused. "Do you remember talking with Trisha Heidkamp yesterday?"

He squinted. "I think so."

"Well, you invited her to go swimming at your heated indoor pool sometime and told her to bring the whole family."

Gordon's eyes widened. "Really?"

"Yeah. I'm sure you weren't thinking, but since you asked," she said as her voice trailed off.

"Okay. Thanks for letting me know. I'll make a point to apologize to her."

She slipped out of the room without another word.

Gordon rubbed his face with both hands as he leaned back in his chair again. Trisha's son drowned four months ago in her hot tub. It was a tough few weeks in the office as Trisha and plenty of other workers shed tears with her.

He pulled out a piece of paper and made a note.

*This isn't going to be as easy as I thought.*

# CHAPTER 8

"WE NEED TO TALK," Banks said as she grabbed Flynn by the back of his collar and forced him down the hall. He went willingly, though not as fast as Banks preferred. He stumbled after a few steps until she released him at the threshold of her office.

Flynn scooted inside and turned around to watch Banks slam the door behind her and storm around her desk. He sat down gingerly.

Banks slammed her first on the table. "What do you think you're doing?"

Flynn shrugged. "My job?" He paused. "I'm not quite sure why you're upset."

"Don't play dumb with me," she said as she rested on her knuckles while leaning over her desk. "I've agreed to let you tag along on this case because I think your expertise could be helpful—but it's not helpful when you write stories like the one you just wrote. We need to control the information that gets out of here so we can control the investigation. If the wrong piece of information slips out, it may give our thief the advantage he needs to elude us or get rid of potential evidence." She paused and then waved dismissively at him. "You already know all that—and I shouldn't have to be here telling you this."

Flynn nodded. "Can I make it up to you by taking you out to dinner tonight?"

She rolled her eyes and sighed. "The only dinner I'll be eating tonight is take out. And you as well, if you want to stick around and be helpful. We've got a lot ground to cover, and fast."

Flynn was pleased with his ability to avoid further trouble with Banks, especially since he didn't even have to use his nuclear option—what Coleman had told him. At least not yet anyway.

He smiled at her. "Whatever you need."

"Grab your coat. We need to get started."

***

THEIR DRIVE TO THE Nisqually National Wildlife Refuge, where early eyewitness reports of a man parachuting out of a plane correlated with the time of the plane being robbed, was largely uneventful—and unfruitful. However, it had taken several days for the tips to roll in and the FBI to ascertain the landing zone, and the scene appeared cold when it came to evidence.

Flynn tried to press Banks for her best theories on *who* and, more importantly, *why*. Flynn insisted that the *why* of a crime always led to the *who*, particularly in the conspiracy cases he'd covered. By the end of the drive, it was clear to Flynn that Banks was truly starting at ground zero on this case.

But Chase Jones, Banks' partner for the investigation, was full of ideas about *why* and *who*. In the backseat, he leafed through a folder full of documents detailing people who'd made threats in the past against the government from both the San Francisco and Seattle areas.

"Wait a minute," Flynn said. "How exactly did the Seattle field office get to take the lead on this case? What about San Francisco?"

"Technically, the crime was committed here, so we get to take the lead," Banks said. "We're working closely with the San Francisco office. But all the evidence is here—the money, the plane, the suspect."

"We're not sure about the suspect," interrupted Jones. "He could be anywhere by now. Maybe even in Canada, if he's smart."

Banks pulled into the parking lot and stopped. She leaned over her shoulder and shot Jones a look. "Let's stick to facts, not conjecture. He could still be in this park for all we know. We don't need to turn this into an international manhunt yet."

They got out of the car and Flynn slapped Jones on the back. "Something tells me this case is more about the thrill than the loot. And thrill seekers like attention."

Jones shrugged. "Maybe. Time will tell."

Banks led the way as they ambled down a dirt path where a Bureau forensics team was already at work.

"Over here, Agent Banks," one of the forensics team members said.

She hustled toward the team with Flynn and Jones in tow.

Oswald Copperfield worked a quarter through his fingers, muttering something unintelligible.

"Oswald?" Banks said.

He snapped out of his stupor. "Oh, yes, Agent Banks.

Sorry. The only thing we've been able to find is what we believe are the suspect's boot prints. These prints begin right here after what appears to be a hard landing over here. And then there are these marks in the mud that would be consistent with a parachute getting drug along the ground." He stood up and walked a few feet. "From all indications, it looks like he gathered up his parachute about right here." He pointed at a spot on the ground where the drag marks vanished.

"Good work, Copperfield" Banks said. "Keep me posted if you find anything else. I'm going to canvas the area."

Flynn surveyed the scene. The selection of Nisqually as a landing spot seemed odd as well as dangerous in the dark.

"Why here?" Flynn asked aloud.

"Low visibility, easy access to public transportation."

Then a train whistle echoed across the water.

Flynn pointed at the train. "Forget public transportation when you can take a train."

The train crawled along, running parallel to the refuge's shoreline for a short distance.

"That's where I'd go," Flynn said.

"Well, that line doesn't leave the country," Banks said. "It ends in Seattle."

Flynn punched Jones playfully. "I guess that destroys your international fugitive idea."

"Maybe," Jones said. "There are plenty of ways to get out of the country without getting detected."

"But not that many so quickly," Banks said. "By air is the only way and we've got agents already looking over flight manifests for international flights originating out of Seattle. Besides, if he wanted to fly out of here, he'd have to leave most of his money behind."

Flynn nodded. "He's still in the area. I'm sure of it."

They continued to talk about the possible exit points and the reason why the suspect chose this landing site over others. While they were discussing this, a plane soared overhead.

"Well, that plane is below ten thousand feet," Flynn said, pointing upward. "That's one reason why this would be a great place to land."

Before anyone could respond, Copperfield yelled for Banks. "We've got something you need to see," he said.

"What is it?" Banks asked as she ran toward him.

"We found his parachute."

# CHAPTER 9

THE SEATTLE-TACOMA International Airport hummed with the usual level of activity, so much so that nobody noticed the hangar cordoned off and surrounded by FBI forensics vans. Coleman flashed the FBI badge he'd lifted from the field office to the officer at the gate entrance. The guard waved him through and directed him to a nearby parking lot for employees. Coleman parked and headed straight for the crime scene.

Memories flooded him as he strode across the tarmac toward the hangar—and most of them weren't good feelings. Failing to find Cooper's body hindered his career advancement. He should've been a Division Chief or Section Chief, but he could never rise above Special Agent in Charge. No matter where he went, he could hear the whispers behind his back. He'd catch people staring at him then looking away.

*This must be how people with disabilities feel.*

It served as a constant source of pain, but one he learned to live with. As he looked at the gray Seattle sky, he smiled. He was going to put this debacle behind him once and for all—even if he never got a single mention of credit. The Bureau would know. *He* would know.

Once he arrived on site, one of the agents put his hand up. "Sir, you can't come in here."

Coleman shoved his hand in his pocket to fish out his badge, thinking up a plausible lie quickly. Then he saw an old friend.

"Steve? Steve Watson? Is that you?" he called.

Steve Watson was a rookie agent during Coleman's final year with the Bureau, an agent with whom Coleman had some rapport.

"Harold? What in the world are you doing out here?" he said, gesturing for the agent to let him through.

Coleman waddled toward Watson. "Well, I wanted to see if I could lend a hand to the investigation."

"And Thurston said it was okay?"

Coleman waved dismissively. "Oh, you know Thurston. He's not big on outside help."

"Well, you're certainly not outside help on this case."

"I guess it depends on how you look at it."

"Why don't you come take a look and tell me what you see? You were always good at inspecting a scene a second time and finding something I missed."

A grin crept across Coleman's face. "If you insist."

"I do."

Coleman headed toward the plane with an extra pep in his step; Watson hustled to keep up.

"So, what are we looking at here?" Coleman asked.

"From what we can tell, this guy basically stowed away in the aft cargo hold of this jet and leapt out right as the plane was making its approach into Sea-Tac."

"Obviously, he had to know about the money beforehand?"

"Absolutely. This wasn't dumb luck, that's for sure."

"A precision strike from someone with the know-how,

the means, and the brazenness to pull it off."

"Exactly." Watson paused. "But not a trace of DNA."

"Which means you've got no suspect?"

"Sounds familiar, huh?"

"Well, would I enjoy watching a new team of Bureau agents being saddled with solving an unsolvable crime just like I was more than forty years ago? I'm not exactly wired that way. I want to see justice, just like I wanted with D.B. Cooper—though I'm sure Mother Nature exacted her justice on him." He took a deep breath and climbed the ladder leading into the aft cargo hold. "But this guy? I'm betting he got away."

Watson gestured toward the plane. "Well have a look inside and tell me what I'm missing."

Coleman poked his head in and stared at the vast space beneath the plane. It certainly wouldn't make for the most comfortable ride, but it was manageable, especially on such a short flight from San Francisco.

"And all he took was a million dollars?" Coleman finally asked.

"Yep," Watson answered. "As far as we can tell."

Coleman climbed inside and started to feel around. He felt between the crevices—and nothing. He was about to climb out when a glint of something caught his eye.

Wedged into a small crack, he saw something Watson's team had missed—a golf ball marker. It was small and its coloring looked like that of the silvery floor. It'd be easy to miss, for sure. He reached for it and sprung it free. Watson couldn't see what he was doing—and he decided against revealing his find to his friend.

"What did you see?" Watson asked.

"Maybe it's my old age—or maybe you're just damn good at scouring a crime scene, but I didn't find anything." He clenched his fist with the marker in his left hand as he worked the marker between two of his fingers and out of sight.

Watson let out a long breath. "Well, it was worth a shot."

Coleman climbed out and found his way to the ground. "I appreciate you giving me the chance to poke around." He offered his hand to Watson. "I just hope you guys catch the bastard."

"You and me both."

Coleman bid his friend goodbye and headed back toward the parking lot.

He glanced down at the marker in his hand and read the name stamped on it: "The Ridgeline Golf and Polo Club."

Finally, he had a promising lead—and he couldn't wait to unearth a suspect and rub Thurston's face in it.

# CHAPTER 10

GORDON DUG HIS BOOTS into Champion's sides and urged his horse forward. "Come on, girl," he said. "We got this." He bore down on the ball and struck it with his mallet, sending it flying through the goalposts for a score.

"Nice strike," Edwin Goodyear said as he galloped by. "Where was that during yesterday's scrimmage? You looked like a drunk man swatting at flies."

Gordon rolled his eyes and guided Champion back to his team's side of the field.

"Really? A drunk man swatting at flies?" Gordon asked as he flitted past Goodyear.

After the throw-in to restart play, Gordon beat everyone to the ball and walloped it through the goal posts again for another score.

He trotted past Goodyear. "Must've been an off day," he quipped. He stopped Champion. "How many goals have you scored again?" He didn't wait for an answer, digging his heels into the side of Champion and leading her back to the other half of the field with his teammates.

Gordon looked toward the stands and eyed Samantha Preston, a mid-20s debutante who seemed above the spoiled "selfie" culture that permeated most of the younger crowd at the polo cub. He determined she was different—she wouldn't be caught dead with a cell phone in her hand.

"Too many germs," she said once to him when he asked her about her aversion to modern technology. "If I wanted to get sick, I'd take my gloves off and open every door in an elementary school." She shooed him away. "Run along now."

Undaunted, Gordon held out an open hand, an obvious gesture that he wanted to kiss hers.

"Perhaps you're denser than you look, though I'm not sure that's possible." She forced a smile and returned her gaze to the field, surveying it for a more acceptable suitor.

He eyed her closely. "What? You're above a kiss on the hand from the best player here at Ridgeline?"

She didn't acknowledge his comment, holding her gaze onto the field.

Gordon felt out of his league when he was around her. Though he'd amassed a small fortune, he knew it would never be enough to keep Ms. Preston satisfied. He needed a large empire to appease her, if only for a week or two. But it didn't stop him from dreaming that she'd turn into a down-to-earth woman and decide that she didn't need a fortune to find love—or a thick tuft of hair either.

*What does it matter? I won't be around much longer anyway.*

Goodyear rode up next to him. "Don't even think about it," he said. "She's all mine. Besides, she's not too fond of men who are long in the tooth."

Gordon glared at Goodyear as he rode away. He felt like mistaking Goodyear's head for the ball. A quick mallet strike and—

He snapped back to reality and returned to his side of the field.

"Wish you would've played like that in the sixth chukker yesterday instead of a ham-fisted rookie," Goodyear yelled at Gordon.

Gordon's eyes narrowed. He led Champion close to the ball and drew back to hit the ball, striking it with precision. A few seconds later, he drove the ball through the goal posts for another score.

Gordon pulled up next to Goodyear. "Don't discount me because of my age, young chap. Rich older men always get the young beautiful women."

Goodyear laughed. "Not older gentlemen that look like they just walked off the set of Men in Black." He paused. "Besides, those sun glasses aren't doing you any favors, unless you prefer to have your giant forehead accentuated."

Without hesitating, Gordon leapt off his horse and tackled Goodyear. The two men tumbled to the ground. Gordon dished out a few hard licks before several other players broke them apart.

Goodyear scraped away a trickle of blood from around the corner of his mouth. He eyed Gordon. "Where'd you learn to hit like that? Some boarding school for girls?"

Gordon stood up and brushed off the dirt on his pants. "The shiner over your eye suggests I hit plenty hard. Hope you don't have any speaking engagements this week, pretty boy."

Gordon then spun and walked off the field, leading Champion by the reins. A few yards away, Goodyear shrieked as he realized his face looked like it had been battered. Champion looked behind her at the scene.

"Don't pay him any attention, girl," Gordon said as he

leaned forward and spoke into Champion's ear. "He's just another drama queen."

As he neared the stands, he noticed Samantha smiling coyly at him. He touched the front of his helmet visor, a tip of a cap to her.

She stood up as he drew closer. "Next time, give him two black eyes," she said. "And do it for every lady here at the club."

Gordon nodded and kept walking, trying hard not to let the smile that had swept across his face morph into a goofy grin. He looked down in an effort to keep his countenance from betraying him.

And while it was a nice distraction from all the inner stress he was attempting to manage, Gordon still had business to attend to—business that he hadn't realized required his attention until his trip to the club.

He handed Champion off to one of the stable hands and slipped a $10 bill into his hand. The kid sneered as he reluctantly pocketed the money.

"Yesterday a $100; today a $10?" the college-aged kid said. "Did I do something wrong?"

"Mind your manners, boy," Gordon said. He balled up his fist and shook it at him. "Maybe tomorrow I'll give you a plain old five."

The stable hand jerked Champions' reins and led her into the stable, glaring over his shoulder at Gordon.

Gordon took off his gloves and hustled toward the clubhouse where he changed and headed back to his car. He fished a burner cell phone out of his gym bag and dialed a number.

"We need to talk about yesterday."

# CHAPTER 11

WITHOUT PUBLISHING ANY ARTICLE to draw Banks' ire, Flynn's Thursday morning got off to a much smoother start—and a promising one at that, moments after entering the FBI's Seattle field office. He decided to not only bring Banks a latte but also a turkey and cheese croissant from a 24-hour diner near the office. While Flynn wasn't initially sure if she'd appreciate his gesture, her wide eyes told him all he needed to know.

"You sure do know how to get out of the dog house," she said as she took his peace offering. She then cocked her head to one side. "But I don't know if that's a good thing or a bad thing?"

"Oh?" he said.

"Yeah, the only men I've ever met who are so adept at making up for their missteps are the ones who seem to make so many."

Flynn's eyebrows shot upward. "No one ever accused me of being smooth." He paused. "Now handsome, on the other hand—"

She rolled her eyes and slapped him on his left bicep, grabbing hold of it. "Save your charm for the starry-eyed twenty-somethings who've been drinking for a few hours. It's not going to work on me, especially before I've had some caffeine and my breakfast."

Flynn took a deep breath. "Can't a man do something nice for a woman without it being considered hitting on someone?"

"So you were hitting on me?"

"I didn't say that. I try to be charming with everyone I meet."

Before Banks could respond, a woman analyst walked near them in the hall and abruptly stopped. "Aren't you James Flynn?" she asked.

Flynn smiled and nodded. He offered his hand. "And you are?"

"Priscilla Westover—one of your biggest fans."

"It's nice to meet you, Priscilla."

"I loved your book on the Fort Knox conspiracy."

Flynn reached inside his bag and pulled out a pad and pen. He handed it to her. "Write down your address and I'll send you a signed copy."

He glanced up at Banks in time to see her roll her eyes.

Banks exhaled a long breath. "Hustle it up, Priscilla. We've got work to do—and I suppose you do too."

Flynn took back his pad after she finished and stuffed it into his backpack, but not before noticing Priscilla had also included her phone number and a smiley face.

"Don't think you're special," Banks said. "Priscilla gives out her number to every male with a pulse."

"Do I detect a hint of jealousy, Agent Banks?"

She rolled her eyes. "Let's go see if forensics has anything for us. Jones said he'd meet us there."

Flynn followed Banks down the hall and up a stairwell to the Forensics Department.

"So this is where the magic happens," Flynn said as he entered the double doors.

"I'd hardly call it magic," Jones said, catching Flynn off guard. "Just because our forensics team leader has the last name of Copperfield doesn't mean he's actually a magician."

Copperfield stepped into the hallway. "Nor does it mean I can make fingerprints appear out of thin air, but I do have some news for you," he said, garnering the attention of all the agents. "But let's hurry. Procrastination is the thief of time."

He spun and headed toward another set of double doors with all the agents trailing behind him. Once inside his lab, he stood behind a table with the parachute laid out on it.

"Unfortunately, I wasn't able to even glean any touch of DNA off this chute," Copperfield said.

"Unbelievable," Jones muttered.

"Truly," Copperfield said, holding up his index finger. "Which means that our thief used gloves whenever he handled this material."

Banks' head dropped. She rubbed her forehead and sighed. "Do you have any good news for us?"

Copperfield smiled. "I'm glad you asked because I did locate a small identifying mark sewn into the parachute itself, a thin strip of cloth with the name of a supply shop on it— Go Ahead, Jump."

"That's the name of the store?" Flynn asked.

Copperfield nodded. "And located on Halen Street." He smiled. "Someone there has a good sense of humor." He handed Banks a sheet of paper and several photos. "Here's the address and some pictures to show the store employees."

"You're a genius, Copperfield," Banks said as she headed toward the exit holding the piece of paper in the air.

"Thanks, but I'm just a man on a mission," Copperfield said.

"Aren't we all?" Jones said.

Flynn shook his head and looked back at Copperfield. "It's a shame to waste your Van Halen reference on such a simpleton."

"Where have all the good times gone?" Copperfield said.

Flynn laughed and backed out of the room, pointing at Copperfield. "You're good. I'm sure we'll see you soon."

\*\*\*

WHEN FLYNN ENTERED Go Ahead, Jump, he was mesmerized by the stunning photography on the wall. Pictures of jumpers soaring over scenic vistas filled every space on the wall not covered by a product display shelf.

Banks nudged Flynn. "Makes you wanna jump out of an airplane, doesn't it?"

He shook his head. "I've done that plenty of times before, but rarely on my own volition."

She shot him a look. "You're kidding, right?"

Flynn said nothing.

"I'll take that as a no."

Flynn nodded. "So, do you like to hurl yourself toward the ground at ridiculous speeds for *fun*?"

"Did it once. Wasn't a fan."

"That fun, huh?"

She smiled. "So, what do you think shopping here says about our thief?"

Flynn shrugged. "Not sure yet, but it's not a place an amateur would go, that's for sure. Anyone wanting to remain anonymous wouldn't come in here and start asking for equipment like a newbie to the hobby. That'd make the person memorable."

She nodded in agreement. "Why don't you join me and Jones while we question the owner?"

"Let's do it."

Jones introduced himself to the store owner, Dell Young. The two men shook hands as Jones introduced Flynn and Banks.

"So, Mr. Young, are you here all the time?"

"Only when I'm not jumping out of airplanes," he said in a raspy voice. He reached for a bottle of water and took a swig. "What's this about, anyway?"

Banks laid a few pictures out on the counter. "Do you recognize this parachute?"

Young leaned over and squinted at the pictures before nodding. "It's a common chute, more for intermediate jumpers. We sell quite a few of those."

"And do you sew your company's tag into all of your chutes?" Jones asked.

Young nodded. "Every last one of them. We want them to see it every time they pack their chute. It's a marketing thing. You know how marketing experts say a person has to see something seven times before they take action? That's our way of putting our name out in front of people at least seven times to make sure they come back here and shop again."

"But you're the only parachute shop in Tacoma," Jones said.

Young took another drink of water. "Seattle's got several of them, too. When you're not the only game in town, you have to be proactive or you'll become irrelevant."

"So would it be safe to say you're here quite a bit?" Banks asked.

"Ask my ex-wife that question," he quipped. "She might've believed me when I told her I wasn't cheating on her if I hadn't been at this store practically every moment it was open." He paused. "What's this all about, anyway?"

Banks sighed. "Did you see the news about the guy who tried to copycat D.B. Cooper?"

"Of course." He gasped. "Did he use one of our parachutes?"

Jones pointed at him. "You're quick."

"I can't believe this," Young said. "I can't imagine who this could be. We sell so many of this model—both new and used."

"Perhaps I can help narrow it down for you," Banks said, sliding the pictures to him again. "We couldn't find a single hair or identifying mark of any kind that would point us to who might have used this chute."

"And you're hoping I can help you?" Young asked in a mocking tone.

"Think, Mr. Young," Flynn said. "Not a single fingerprint. Do you remember anyone who came in here wearing gloves?"

Young furrowed his brow and thought for a moment. "Well, there was this one guy who came in a few months ago who was memorable, if only for the fact that he was dressed like a horse jockey. Problem was he looked to be nearly six feet tall. I thought all those guys who raced horses were short and tiny."

"Would you happen to remember when?" Banks asked.

"Hmm. Maybe three or four months ago."

Jones looked up and pointed at the security camera. "Do you still have the footage?"

Young shook his head. "We recycle those tapes every thirty days. You won't find him on there, I guarantee you that."

"Think, Mr. Young," Banks said. "This is extremely important. Do you remember any other details about him? Did he perhaps pay with a credit card?"

Young shook his head. "I'm pretty sure he paid with cash, which is also an oddity around here, especially considering all the high-dollar items we sell." He paused. "But I think I know where he worked."

"And where's that?"

Young closed his eyes and banged his fist on the counter. "Oh, where was it?" He threw his head back. "He was a banker somewhere." He snapped his fingers. "It was—it was—oh, yes—Bank of Olympia." He held up his index finger. "He mentioned he was in finance and I remember seeing a credit card with Bank of Olympia on it when he put the change back in his wallet."

"So you're not sure that's where he worked?" Jones asked.

"Well, the large number of crisp $100 bills seemed a bit unusual to me. It's not like ATMs spit out crisp bills every time—or maybe he was stealing money back then."

Banks shook her head. "Doubtful." She offered her hand to Mr. Young. "Thank you for your time. You've been extremely helpful."

The trio exited the shop and got into Banks' car.

Banks sighed before turning the ignition. "Well, that was a positive development. Now we only have to sift through the hundred or so Bank of Olympia personnel files to figure out who the mystery man was that purchased the parachute—and it still may not be him."

Flynn snickered. "That'll take far too long."

"And you have another idea?" Jones asked.

Flynn nodded. "Where can you play polo around here?"

# CHAPTER 12

HAROLD COLEMAN PULLED off the highway and onto the long cobblestone driveway that led to the Victorian-style clubhouse situated atop a small hill overlooking a large swath of private property. To the left, a slew of properly attired golfers hacked at balls on the driving range. To the right, several fields of manicured grass sprawled up to a line of stables. Along the road, ornate lampposts situated about every twenty yards apart added to the otherworldly charm of the surroundings.

This wasn't the first time Coleman had been on the premises of the Ridgeline Golf and Polo Club, but he hoped it was the last.

He stopped his modest silver Toyota Camry just in front of the valet podium outside the clubhouse.

"Joining us for lunch?" asked a young man wearing a polo shirt with the club's insignia.

"Depends on how things go," Coleman answered as he stood up.

The young man tore a receipt off the claim ticket and handed it to Coleman. "Enjoy your time here, sir."

Coleman climbed the steps of the clubhouse and put his hands on his hips. He glanced around at the beautiful scenery, Mount Rainier ascending to glorious heights in the distance. It wasn't as green as he'd remembered, but it was still picturesque.

*Damn rich people.*

He reversed course and struck out toward the polo fields, heading straight for the stables. It took him a few minutes to reach the structure tucked neatly against the tree line. Once there, he stopped for a few moments to catch his breath.

*I've gotta stop smoking.*

While obviously out of place, his presence near the stables didn't seem to alarm anyone. Several stable hands nodded politely at him as they led horses down the stable or carted buckets of water around the building. But Coleman knew they couldn't show they were leery of him, even if they were. The hired hands were trained to respect everyone and be polite in every circumstance—that's how you got fat tips and stomached working around such pompous blowhards. At least, that's how Coleman perceived things.

After he caught his breath, he grabbed one of the stable hands as he walked by.

"I was wondering if you could help me," Coleman said. "I'm trying to find one of your polo players."

"There are plenty of them milling around on the field still," the young man said.

"I mean a specific one."

"Gotta name? I know almost all of them."

"Actually, a name is what I'm looking for."

The stable hand cocked his head to one side and stared at Coleman. "Are you supposed to be back here?"

"Look, I know you're busy. Just carry on."

The young man shook his head and walked off. He

glanced back over his shoulder at Coleman.

Coleman walked around the corner and found another young man pushing a wheelbarrow full of hay toward the entrance of the stable.

"Excuse me, young man. May I have a moment of your time?" Coleman asked.

The man stopped and dropped the wheelbarrow handles. "What can I help you with, sir?"

"I'm trying to locate one of your polo players."

"If you've got a name, I could point him out to you."

Coleman took a deep breath. "You see, that's just it. I don't know his name and I'm trying to find him."

"Do you know what he looks like?"

"That's the other thing."

The stable hand picked up the wheelbarrow handles. "Sir, you're going to be difficult to help and I've got work to do. Wish I could help." He scurried off around the corner, disappearing into the stable.

Coleman closed his eyes, made a fist and repeatedly tapped his forehead with it.

*Think, Coleman. Think.*

Another young man came by with a horse in tow. "Can I help you, sir?"

Coleman opened his eyes and looked up. "I hope so. I'm looking for someone who plays polo here at the club."

"Does this person have a name? I know everyone here."

"Not a name that I know—but a personality, a reckless personality."

The stable hand furrowed his brow. "I'm afraid you'll have to be more specific, mister. Most people here like to live on the edge."

"I'm not talking about reckless as in driving fast Italian sports car—I'm talking about wild and crazy, unpredictable even. The kind of person who seems erratic and you never know what they're going to do from one day to the next. Maybe even the kind who jumps out of airplanes one day and plays polo the next."

The stable hand laughed and nodded. "I know exactly who you're talking about."

"And who exactly is that?"

The stable hand didn't open his mouth or even move. His eyebrows shot upward, giving a knowing look to Coleman, who took a few seconds to figure out what was happening. Coleman dug into his pocket and jammed a $20 bill into the man's hand.

"As I was saying, the man you're looking for is Carlton Gordon. He's a bit of an enigma around here. He works at a bank, but nobody knows where his real money comes from. Sometimes, he can be quite the—"

"What's going on here?" an older gentleman snapped as he walked up on Coleman and the young man talking. "Mr. Hunter, this is your place of employment, not a social club. I suggest you put up Mr. Gordon's horse and be about your business."

The stable hand's head dropped as he shuffled off with the horse.

The older man turned toward Coleman. "As for you, sir. I'm not sure who you think you are snooping around our stables or what you're doing here, but these places are off limits to everyone but employees. And last I checked, you weren't working for me here at Ridgeline."

Coleman nodded. "Sorry. I didn't mean to—"

"Didn't mean to what? Interrupt my employees doing their jobs?" He took a deep breath. "What are you doing here, anyway?"

"I was looking for someone and I—"

The man stamped his foot. "Do you even belong to the club?"

"No, I—"

"And you just thought you could waltz on over here and start interrogating my employees."

Coleman dug into his pocket and fished out his badge. "I'm working an undercover sting operation for the FBI, if you must know."

The older man put his hands on his hips and shook his head. "I don't believe you. Who's your supervisor?"

"Director Thurston."

"Excellent. So, if I call Director Thurston, he'll vouch for you?"

"Well, I—"

The old man pulled a cellphone out of his pocket. "What's the director's number?"

"He's not in right now."

"And how do you know that?"

"He's attending a conference in D.C. this week."

The old man looked back at his phone and started dialing a number.

"What are you doing?" Coleman demanded.

"I'm calling the authorities. I'll let you sort it out with them—but I'm most certainly not going to let you wait around our stables while they do."

Coleman shook his head. "Sir, that's not necessary."

"It's not necessary if I want to remain stupid. But I

prefer the truth—and you haven't been honest with me from the moment we started talking."

Coleman decided he didn't want to wait another minute while his freedom—and credibility—hung in the balance. He started to head off across the polo fields back toward the valet stand.

"Don't you walk away from me," the old man snarled. "I'm not done with you yet."

But Coleman was done with him—and everyone else at the club. However, he didn't get far before the old man hustled up behind him, ordering him to stop.

"Are you listening to me? I said 'stop'!"

Coleman stopped and spun around. "I'm sorry to have wasted your time, sir." He had what he wanted—no need to be belligerent and draw more attention.

*Just keep walking.*

This time, Coleman increased his pace as much as he could with his cane.

"Don't walk away from me, mister."

Coleman ignored him, pressing toward his car.

"Stop, right now!"

In a matter of seconds, two polo players positioned their horses in front of Coleman and boxed him in. Coleman scuttled to the side in an attempt to get around them, but he couldn't find an opening as the players directed their horses to stay in front of him.

For about a minute, this dance continued until Coleman finally threw his hands in the air.

"Geez. What do you want from me? I'm leaving," Coleman said.

"You bet you are," the old man said. "And you're

leaving in the back of a squad car." He pointed toward the club's driveway where a pair of patrol cars roared onto the property.

The two cars stopped along the edge and sprinted across the field, where the old man was waving his arms up and down.

*Oh, geez. A pair of hotshot uniforms.*

"On the ground, now," one of the officers yelled as he approached Coleman.

Coleman complied with their order, but it didn't stop the men from handling him roughly and slapping a pair of handcuffs on him.

They dragged Coleman to his feet and pushed him forward toward their patrol car.

"You realize you're dealing with an FBI agent, right?" Coleman said.

"Show me that badge and I'll cut you loose," one of the officer's said.

"I don't have it with me."

The officer rolled his eyes. "Well, good luck explaining that to the chief—or anyone else. The club doesn't take too kindly to people trespassing. This is a private club, you know."

Coleman lumbered forward, mostly at the behest of the other officer standing behind him to make sure he kept pace with the fleet-footed man leading the way.

"You should be scared, old man," the officer in front said. "Our chief works closely with prosecutors on all cases related to the Ridgeline Golf and Polo Club—especially since he's a member out there."

"It was all a big misunderstanding," Coleman said.

"Like hell it was. You better be very afraid of what's coming your way," the other officer snapped.

Coleman wasn't afraid of what they'd do to him.

If truth be told, he was more afraid his wife would forbid him from working on this case—and solving it was all that mattered to him.

# CHAPTER 13

FLYNN STARED OUT HIS WINDOW, eyes widening as he surveyed the scene unfolding near the Ridgeline Golf and Polo Club clubhouse. The towering beauty of the Northwest Pines went unnoticed due to the flashing lights. Flynn strained to see the perp but couldn't make out his face.

"Somebody must've forgotten to pay up after losing a bet on the golf course," Jones quipped from the backseat.

"I would've thought they'd handle such situations far more discreetly here," Banks said. "My family belonged to a country club once and situations were taken care of in a much more diplomatic manner."

Flynn broke his gaze and snapped his head toward Banks. "You? Country club? You were born with a silver spoon in your mouth?"

"It was Valleydale, Mississippi. If you could rub two nickels together, you could join," she said.

"Unless you were black," Jones said.

"Valleydale may have been at the center of several historic civil rights moments in the 60s, but that's not how I remember it," she said.

"Of course not," Jones said. "It's hard to tell what's really going on when you're sitting in a rocking chair on one of those giant plantation home porches."

She glared at Jones. "It wasn't like that—and I certainly didn't grow up with a silver spoon in my mouth—or a bronze-plated one either."

"Fair enough," Flynn said as he reached across and put his hand on Banks' knee. "Don't get so defensive. Besides, we've got an investigation to do."

Banks pulled her door handle and put her shoulder into the window, flinging the door open.

The valet hustled toward her and held out his hand for the key. She handed it to him and didn't look back as she strode toward the clubhouse door.

Flynn punched Jones in the arm and said in a low voice, "Go easy on her. People can't help where they're from."

Jones rolled his eyes and scampered up the steps after Banks.

Flynn stopped at the top step and paused before entering the building. He looked once more at the squad car that was now leaving the premises. Whoever was inside would remain a mystery to him. He spun on his heels and opened the door.

He hustled to catch up with Banks, who'd already located someone to help her. She appeared animated as she put one hand on her hips and the other she used to gesture wildly.

*Note to self: Don't make clichéd jokes about Mississippi to Banks.*

As he neared Banks and Jones, Flynn caught enough of the tail end of the conversation to learn that a manager was being contacted to help them.

Flynn decided to make small talk while they waited.

"So, what happened to your accent?"

Banks laughed and shook her head. "It vanished a long time ago, mostly by my own doing."

"Why's that?" Flynn asked.

"Do you ever take a woman serious who speaks with a slow Southern drawl?"

Jones launched into a story. "I met a girl from Jackson once and—"

"Enough with you and your Mississippi stories, Jones," Banks snapped. "I'm not taking them serious at all, not to mention I have a hard time believing any girl from Jackson would give you the time of day."

"Someone did not get enough sleep last night," Jones shot back.

"I'm gonna give you a big piece of my mind accompanied by my fist if you keep this up," she said.

Jones put his hands up in surrender. "Okay, okay. Fine. I'll leave you and lover boy in peace. Besides, I don't even know what he's doing here or why anyone ever approved him."

Flynn's eyes narrowed. "Just keep talkin' if you want to find out what I'm capable of."

Banks scowled but flashed a quick wink at Flynn. "Let's focus on the case, fellas."

A few awkward moments of silence followed until a club manager approached.

"Henry Elberton," he said, offering his hand. He exchanged names with each one as they shook his hand. "Welcome to the Ridgeline Golf and Polo Club, though I doubt you ever expected to be here under such circumstances."

"I never expected to be here at all," Jones said.

Elberton forced a smile. "Very well, then. How can I help you?"

"We're looking for a suspect—a male in his mid-40s, dark hair, a bit of a receding hairline on top, about five-ten or five-eleven, maybe six feet tall. Know of anyone like this?"

Elberton laughed and clasped his hands together. "I'm afraid you're going to need to be more specific than that if you want my help. That description matches about thirty percent of the men here." He paused. "May I ask what this is concerning?"

"It's concerning a crime," Banks said.

"What kind of crime? The clientele here isn't exactly a group of hardened criminals."

"More specifically, a robbery," Banks answered.

"A robbery? Now I'm afraid you're looking in the wrong location. If any crimes are committed here, it's of the white collar variety."

"Are you sure?" Jones said. "This is the kind of robbery where you strap a million dollars to you and jump out of an airplane."

Elberton shook his head emphatically. "Definitely not here."

"*Definitely?* You sound so sure," Jones said.

"Agent Jones, this is not the kind of establishment for men who commit such shenanigans—or women, for that matter. Most members here make more in one week than you make in a year. They have no desire to risk their wealth on such frivolity, much less their lives. I can assure you that whatever pointed you in this direction is mistaken."

Elberton stopped and took a deep breath. He stared

at all of them cautiously, eyeing each one with suspicion.

"Can I see your badges?" he asked.

Banks nodded and flipped open the small wallet containing her FBI identification. Jones did the same.

"And you sir?" Elberton asked as he looked at Flynn.

"I'm consulting on this case," Flynn said.

Banks nodded. "Yes, I'll vouch for him. He's a consultant."

"I wish I could be of more help to you, but I'm afraid I simply can't." Elberton said. "You're just not going to find that type of person around here."

"What about the guy getting shoved into a police car when we drove up?" Flynn said. "He's exactly the kind of person."

"That guy? You must not have taken a good look at his face," Elberton answered.

"His face was shielded a bit."

"If you'd seen his face, you would've known he was an elderly gentleman, who'd clearly began his morning without taking his meds. He even claimed to be FBI as well." Elberton bowed his head and clapped his hands together. "Now, if you don't have anything further, I need to be going. We have a big dinner tonight to prepare for."

Banks handed him her card. "Call me if you think of anything else."

"Will do." Elberton spun and walked swiftly down the hall.

"Well, that got us nowhere," Jones said.

"We need to come back," Flynn said. "Maybe when there's someone else on staff a little more willing to help us—and perhaps a little more open minded as to the criminal potential of the clients here."

"Agreed," Banks said. "But let's get outta here for now."

Outside, the valet jogged up to Banks and handed a set of keys to her. "I've never driven a federal agents' car before."

She laughed. "It's not all it's cracked up to be, is it? No spy gadgets or anything like that."

He smiled. "It was a nice break from the European sports cars."

She handed him a couple of dollars and refused to dig out any more money despite the disappointed look on his face.

They all climbed into Banks' car, Flynn riding shotgun with Jones in the back.

"Well, that was fun," Banks said.

Before anyone could say another word, the sound of glass shattering ripped through the car, along with a bullet that struck the dashboard. Instinctively, they all ducked down as Banks tried to keep her heard just high enough to see the road.

"Maybe we shouldn't come back," Jones shouted.

"This is exactly why we have to," Flynn said.

*Crack!*

Another bullet whistled through the car and struck the back of Flynn's seat.

"Go! Go! Go!" Flynn yelled.

Banks jammed her foot on the gas as the car roared toward the exit. The tires squealed as she yanked the steering wheel and pulled back onto the state highway that kept them hidden from most of civilization.

# CHAPTER 14

THE THICK PINES in the Pacific Northwest served as adequate blinds, something Gordon learned from his father while elk hunting in Idaho as a teenager. He had staked out a position in a tree—similar to the one he was currently in—when he shot his first bull. As he watched the FBI agents swerve onto the state highway and out of sight, a smile crept across his face. He could almost hear his father's voice.

*When you take to higher ground, son, you can see everything as it is in its place—and you can better anticipate the animal's next move.*

Gordon knew that wisdom applied to more than animals.

*You can anticipate people's moves if you have the right perspective.*

For Gordon, this went beyond simply seeing *where* someone was physically. This applied to a person's mental state as well—*what are they thinking?* Gordon didn't have to ask. He knew.

In a way, it wasn't fair, toying with federal investigators in such a manner. He knew what their next move would be—and he'd already set up a way to ensure they would find nothing against him. But then again, why did everything have to be fair. Even if he wasn't operating with a healthy understanding of the human—and law enforcement—psyche, he'd still be several steps ahead of them. FBI investigations were rote as much as they were predictable. He wanted to spice things up and make things far more entertaining, if only for his own benefit. It wasn't exactly how D.B. Cooper went about things, but Gordon didn't care. He wanted to leave his own mark on this case. Despite what the media inferred, he wasn't trying to copy Cooper—just experience what it was like to be him. The rush of stealing the money. The thrill of jumping into an unknown area. The satisfaction of watching the years drip past without getting caught as FBI official after FBI official vowed to unmask the criminal hidden in plain sight.

D.B. Cooper was equally exciting and droll. Exciting because no one had ever baffled the FBI like he did. Droll because he vanished and was never heard from again. America wanted to celebrate this folk hero. People sang songs about him, wrote books about him. Documentaries focused on him. But Cooper was nothing more than an alias, a name ripped from a comic book and used to taunt law enforcement officials from afar.

He climbed down from the tree and collected all his shell casings. He slipped through the pines to his car and pulled onto the road. If only for a moment, his pride in pulling one over on the feds was abated by the twinge of pain in his stomach. *Mission accomplished.*

He'd done exactly what he wanted to do—draw interest in his direction but avoid getting caught.

His phone buzzed with a call from his oncologist. Without answering it, he tossed his phone onto the passenger seat and kept driving. He wasn't going to let more bad news get him down. This was his moment, the first of many he hoped to see played out in the days ahead.

But Gordon didn't dwell on his present victory too long. He had an ending to plan.

# CHAPTER 15

JAMES FLYNN WINCED as he saw the number pop up on the screen of his phone. *Theresa Thompson.* He knew exactly what she was going to say to him—and he didn't want to hear it. Not tonight anyway. He had a quasi date with Jennifer Banks.

If truth be told, it was simply two colleagues getting together over dinner, but he didn't exactly see it that way. He saw it as an opportunity to find out more about this woman, who was as mysterious as she was beautiful. He had a thousand questions he wanted to ask her, partly because he wanted to learn more about her but also because it would distract her from getting to know the real James Flynn. He wasn't even sure who he was any more since he'd left the CIA—and he certainly didn't like the smarmy journalist label. Though it sounded cliché to him, Flynn felt like he was suddenly trying to find himself. Not that he was lost in the world, but he was certainly living a life that appeared to be devoid of purpose. Stopping bad guys seemed like a noble purpose. Writing articles that served as little more than click bait for conspiracy theorist junkies? Where was the purpose in that? He tried not to think about it as he went to sleep each night.

The phone stopped ringing for a moment. Flynn sighed and smiled.

*Disaster averted.*

Before he could move another muscle, the phone rang again—and again, it was Thompson.

*Can't a man get a moment of peace?*

"Hi, Theresa," he said as he answered his phone. "How was your day?"

"I didn't call to chit-chat, Flynn," she snapped. "I want to know when you're going to file something."

"Well, when people stop shooting at me, maybe I can get something together for you."

"Geez, Flynn. You're embedded with the FBI's lead investigative team but you can't seem to get us an update on the hottest story in the country right now?"

Flynn sighed. "Look, I don't want to jeopardize my standing. If I do, I'm out—not just a little bit, but all the way. I haven't been doing this my whole life, but I know not to torch bridges just for a single story."

"Fine. But I need *something*. I don't care what it is—a short update, a story that nothing happened today, anything. This is an ongoing investigation and we need more regular updates."

"That's not my regular schtick, but I'll do my best. You know I'm an investigative reporter, not a news reporter?"

"I know—and I'm wishing I had someone else there about right now."

"I'll file something shortly, but don't expect an earth-shaking story, okay?"

"Just get it to me ASAP."

Flynn hung up and threw the phone on his bed. He

still needed to take a shower—after he returned several phone calls, which undoubtedly were requests for him to be on radio and television programs discussing the investigation.

*Not tonight. I've got a date.*

Technically, it was just dinner with Banks, but he couldn't help himself. It felt like something more. There was chemistry between them—at least, that's how he perceived it. And even if he was only imagining it, there was a unique bond they shared by facing life-threatening situations together, something that had become a regular habit.

Flynn opened his laptop and ripped off a short 300-word update. Nothing new other than to say that the FBI was actively vetting hundreds of tips that had come in on the hotline set up for the case. It was an article that was "mailed in" in more ways than one. It was guaranteed to draw ire from Thompson but keep him in Banks' good graces for the time being—a necessary compromise.

\*\*\*

DINNER AT THE PINK DOOR proved to be a strange experience for Flynn. While he'd read that The Pink Door was one of the most unique restaurants in Seattle, he didn't take the time to investigate what that really meant. Never at any time did he think that meant watching a Ukranian trapeze artist flip around on a swing directly above their table. He simply saw the more than five hundred five-star reviews on Yelp! and decided it must be Seattle's finest.

"Have you been here before?" Flynn asked.

"Once," Banks answered.

He didn't want to dwell on his restaurant choice or the obvious implications of her answer. He preferred to stare at the beautiful woman sitting across the table from him and get to know her more. The fact that their lives weren't on the line was simply a bonus.

"So, why did you join the FBI?" Flynn asked.

She took a deep breath and looked down. "It's a long story."

"I've got time—and no one has me in the sights of their sniper rifle."

She forced a smile and cocked her head to one side. "Are you sure about that?"

He laughed. "Let's hear it."

"Well, when I was eighteen and a freshman in college, my brother, Will, was murdered. Shot dead in an alley by what the police described as a drug deal gone bad. But I knew my brother. He didn't do drugs—ever. He was a choir-boy, literally. He sang in Mass every Sunday at St. Paul's Cathedral. And we were close, always hanging out together. I dated several of his friends just so I could spend more time with him. But they were nerds, guys who were into quantum physics and role play video games. I hated it, but I loved Will and would do anything for him."

"So you wanted to find out what happened to him?"

"Since the local cops wouldn't tell me anything beyond that, I thought it was the only way. I couldn't fathom that he was involved in anything as nefarious as illegal drug use. But when I went through his personal belongings afterward, I found a notebook with all these strange markings and numbers. It seemed like a system of sorts, with dates, but I couldn't make any sense out of it."

"Did you crack it?"

"Not yet, though I've spoken with several leading cryptologists at the Bureau to see if they could point me in the right direction. Nothing yet, but I'm not going to stop until I find out what happened to him."

"All that just to find out who killed your brother?"

She nodded. "And I wouldn't trade a minute of my life since then."

"You're a damn good investigator," Flynn said. "Just know that. We're going to catch this phony copycat—and I bet you'll find out what happened to your brother too. It's just a matter of time."

She smiled again. "Thanks. I appreciate that. My parents think I'm crazy—and I try not to hold it against them that they're not as desperate to know what happened to Will. Some people seem to accept tragedy easier than others."

"Or they deal with it by sticking their head in the sand."

"Sometimes, I wish I would do that."

Flynn shook his head. "Don't ever feel that way. That drive to get to the truth is part of what makes you a good agent. Without people like you, the world would be teeming with crooks and criminals."

A waiter walked up to their table holding a bottle of wine. Without asking a question, he started to pour Banks a glass.

She held her hand up. "I don't think we ordered any wine."

The waiter withdrew the bottle and then poured wine in Flynn's glass. "Right you are, Miss. However, there's a man behind me who sent over this bottle for you."

Banks leaned around the waiter in an effort to see him.

In a dark corner of the restaurant, a man wearing a fedora and glasses touched the brim of his hat and nodded in her direction.

"Who is he?" Banks asked.

The waiter shrugged. "I have no idea. I just do what I'm told, especially when I'm tipped like he tipped me." A faint smile spread across his face.

"Well, tell him thank you for us," Banks said as she raised her glass in a toast.

Flynn followed suit. "To D.B. Cooper," he said with a laugh. "May you stop inspiring criminals to follow in your footsteps."

"Here, here," she said, clinking her glass with his.

They both gulped down the wine.

"That is outstanding," Flynn said, holding the glass in front of him and admiring it.

"I'll drink to that," Banks said, throwing back the glass and draining the wine.

\*\*\*

AFTER DINNER, Flynn stood up and offered his left arm for Banks. She wrapped her right arm around his and walked with him toward the exit. Flynn looked over his shoulder once more to catch a glimpse of the woman flipping around on the trapeze.

"Next time I suggest a Seattle restaurant, let me know if it's also part of a circus," Flynn said.

Banks laughed and let go of his arm to exit the restaurant. As she did, she stumbled and collapsed onto the sidewalk.

Flynn knelt down beside her. "Are you okay?" He

shook her gently. "Jennifer, are you okay?"

She moaned and rolled to her right.

Before Flynn could say another word, a man in a fedora hat rushed over to help.

"What seems to be the problem?" he asked.

"My friend—" Flynn said right before he collapsed on top of her.

# CHAPTER 16

HAROLD COLEMAN KEPT HIS HEAD down as the guard buzzed the door open. He trudged ahead, unwilling to look at Edith and the inevitable disappointment written all over her face. If he had his way, he'd rather her just hit him over the head a few times with her purse and scream at him to get it over with.

He stopped at the desk at the clerk's urging. "Sign here for your personal effects, Mr. Coleman," she said.

He scribbled his name on her clipboard and took the envelope from her before shuffling along. Despite his shame, he had to look up at some point.

When his eyes met Edith's, her anger appeared absent. She forced a smile and put her arm around him.

"Let's get you home, honey," she said.

"I need to get my car. It's still at the Ridgeline Golf and Polo Club."

They remained silent for most of the ride until Edith finally spoke.

"You know I still love you no matter what, right?" she said.

He nodded.

"I just don't understand you sometimes. This case— it's gotten under your skin and you can't let it go."

He grunted. "This case has been under my skin for several decades. It's hardly a new development."

She pulled into the impound lot and put the car in park. "But I've never seen you like this before. What's going on with you?"

"You think I like flipping through the cable channels and hearing people make fun of me, mocking me, breaking down how I ignored the evidence of the most likely suspect?"

She shook her head. "Of course not."

"You're damn right I don't like it. And I'm gonna do something about it."

"But, Harold, it's not worth your life. I don't want to see you going on some foolish crusade to clear your name at the expense of something far more important—your own life. Just ignore those people. They don't know anything. They weren't there."

"Yeah, well, maybe they are right. Maybe I missed it. Maybe D.B. Cooper was right in front of me all along and I failed. Maybe all the criticism is deserved."

"You can't do anything about that now. You're not a part of the Bureau any more and it doesn't matter."

"It matters to me," he screamed. "It matters to me." He started to weep softly.

She put her arm around him. "Harold, the only thing that matters is that you did your best."

He shrugged off her arm. "That's exactly what losers say."

"It's not about winning, Harold. It's about doing the best with what you've got."

"Well, I'm not satisfied with that."

She sighed. "You can't change the past." She patted his knee. "It's been over forty years, Harold. Just accept it and move on."

He took a deep breath and let it out through his teeth. "But I can't. I actually found something that might lead to this copycat being caught."

She rolled her eyes. "You're insufferable."

"Look out!" he screamed as he reached for the wheel.

A deer stood directly in front of them, frozen in the high beams.

The car careened into a ditch, deploying the airbags. Edith didn't appear hurt, but she seemed disoriented, while Coleman escaped unscathed, save a few scratches on his face and hands. He waited a few moments before he inspected her again and didn't see any visible signs of blood loss.

"The club is only a few hundred yards up ahead," he said as he reached over and squeezed her hand. "I'll be back in a few minutes with help. Just sit tight."

Coleman pulled out his cane and hobbled down the road. The pale moon provided enough light for him to see where he was going.

After a five-minute hike, he reached the long cobble-stone driveway leading up to the club. He saw his car sitting in the valet lot.

"Can I help you, sir?" one of the valets asked.

"Actually, you can. I'm picking up my car from earlier today after an unfortunate incident and misunderstanding, but my wife just ran off the road into a ditch while she was swerving to miss a deer about a quarter of a mile back. Perhaps you can call a wrecker for me."

The valet nodded. "This crazy day will just never end."

"Crazy? How so?"

"I take it you're the one who got arrested for attacking one of the stable hands and—"

"Well, I didn't *attack* anyone and—"

"Then someone shot at some FBI agents who were out here conducting an investigation."

"When are those people going to learn?"

The valet furrowed his brow. "Who? The FBI?"

"They keep ignoring me."

"Excuse me. Who are you again?"

Coleman saluted the young man. "Sorry, gotta run. Please don't forget to call the wrecker and give them my number." He dug a business card out of his car and limped over to the valet, handing him the card. "And if you think of anything you saw today that might help us catch the shooter, don't hesitate to call me."

The valet held up the card. "So, you're with the FBI, too?"

"Call me," Coleman said as he slammed the door and fired up the engine. He slammed his foot on the gas and sped away.

*I know who's shooting at them—if only they'll listen to me.*

# CHAPTER 17

GORDON TIGHTENED THE ROPES binding Flynn and Banks to a pole near the wall. They were starting to awaken from the drug he'd put in their bottle of wine a few hours before.

*This ought to do the trick.*

He jammed a needle into Flynn's neck and did likewise with Banks. Both of them moaned and looked at him in bewilderment. This time he didn't want to knock them out—he wanted them awake for the next portion of his show.

Gordon, donning a pair of goggles and a helmet, crouched in front of them, softly slapping both of them in the face to get their attention.

"Wake up, Mr. Flynn," he said, using his voice changer device. It sounded cold and robotic, exactly how Gordon liked it. "Did you enjoy the bottle of wine I sent over?" He threw his head back and laughed, most of it contrived. He wanted to see how much the device tweaked his laughter.

He scooted over and grabbed Banks' chin with his right hand. "And you, Agent Banks—did you enjoy yourself this evening?" She narrowed her eyes and glared at him.

"Why you—"

He wagged his finger at her. "No, no, no. We're not going to be calling each other names tonight. I brought you here for an entirely different reason."

He stood up and walked over toward the wall and flipped a switch. In the center of the room, a large fan with trampoline-type netting affixed over it started to blow.

Gordon returned to his two prisoners. "If you think it's going to be easy to catch D.B. Cooper's twin, think again."

With that, Gordon bounded on top of the trampoline mesh netting and spread his body out prostrate, allowing the wind to carry him upward. He went up and down, putting on a show with several flips and various sky diving maneuvers. As he descended a final time, he remained there for a moment, digging into his pockets. He then flung two fistfuls of $100 bills into the air. The money danced around him as he spun around in the air.

"Isn't this fun?" he asked.

Neither one of them flinched.

Gordon waved dismissively at them. "Oh, don't be such spoil sports. Everyone likes a good hunt, right? I mean, the original D.B. Cooper wasn't nearly this entertaining, was he? He just took his money and hid, but not me. I'm playing with it. See?"

He snatched a bill out of the air and put it in his mouth. With a remote control, he turned off the device and climbed down. He slipped the bill into Banks' hands and did a provocative dance. She didn't move.

Gordon stuck his bottom lip out, yielding a pouty face. "Aren't you going to give me a tip?"

She rolled her eyes at him and threw the money on the floor.

He snatched it up and stuffed it into his pocket.

"Oh, that was your big chance," Gordon said, laughing. "I wanted to see if you'd pocket it and hand it off to forensics. But you didn't. Poor choice. Perhaps you're just as incompetent as the original agent who worked on this case. What's his name again? Something Coleman?" He walked over toward the corner of the room and poured himself a small glass of Scotch. "Ah, what difference does it make? History forgot him, just like they'll forget you once you fail to catch me."

"I will catch you," Banks said through clenched teeth.

Gordon stared at her for a moment. "My, my. Someone sure is confident."

"Confidence is often a preamble to defeat," Flynn chimed in.

"Mr. Flynn speaks," Gordon said. "You must forgive me for not being impressed by your hyperbole there, but I find that simply isn't the case. If you aren't confident, what are you? Scared?"

"In the absence of fear, there is no valor," Flynn snarled.

"What's next, Mr. Flynn? The journey of a thousand miles begins with one step? Do you think pithy one-liners will elevate my opinion of you and let you go?" He took a long pull on his glass of Scotch. "Well, if so, you're right about one thing—I'm going to let you go, but only to keep things interesting. Otherwise, it's all too boring. You see, Cooper planned the perfect crime, but he had no personality. Perhaps he was just a disgruntled airline employee who wanted to hurt the company and was no fun to be around at a party. But that sounds more like a psychopath killer than a thief who doubles as a ghost. I mean, where's the fun in that, right?"

Gordon laughed and walked over toward the table where he opened a leather briefcase and rifled through it.

"Ah-ha! I found you," he said, staring at the syringe.

He sauntered back toward Flynn and Banks, eyeing the medicine inside the vial.

When he glanced down at his pair of prisoners, he saw a healthy dose of fear in their eyes.

"Good, good," Gordon said. "I see that perhaps you two do have valor because I definitely see the fear right now." He paused. "And, no, I'm not changing my mind. I'm still letting you go—but not until you get a small shot."

With that, Gordon jammed the needle into Flynn's neck and released half of the liquid. Then he injected the rest of the vial's contents into Banks' neck.

"Good night, you two."

\*\*\*

THE DRUG WOULD KEEP Flynn and Banks under for another hour or so, just in time for the Seattle workday to get started. Gordon neared the bank and hit a button on a small device in his pocket. He was told that it could disable all video feeds within a half-mile radius.

Once his car came to a stop, he dragged the two bodies from his backseat onto the sidewalk and hoisted them up the steps. He wondered if they might have been a better place to put them, but he decided that his choice was best.

No one would ever suspect him of pulling off such a feat, even if he was right in front of them. He even played out the court scenes in his head. No jury would convict him on such a flimsy case.

Not that it would matter. He didn't expect to be

around long enough to go to trial, even if he somehow managed to get caught.

"Sleep tight," he said, whispering in Banks' ear and pulling a blanket over her. He had snatched a few blankets the last time he served at the homeless shelter. He hadn't done much good over the past few days—past few years, if he was honest. But he never failed to help serve in the soup kitchen every week. It didn't absolve him for his blatant transgressions, but it did assuage his conscience, even if only temporarily.

"See you soon," he whispered in Flynn's ear.

And then he was gone.

# CHAPTER 18

FLYNN OPENED HIS EYES and squeezed them shut, repeating the exercise until he regained his bearings. The right side of his face felt cold and the cacophony of honking cars, screeching tires, and revving engines jolted him awake.

*Where am I?*

He shrugged off a blanket and pushed himself up from the steps. He looked around at the early Friday morning bustle of downtown Seattle. Men and women hustled along the sidewalks, juggling cell phones, briefcases, and coffee cups. The sun reflecting off the glass on the building behind him forced Flynn to shade his eyes.

"Bank of Olympia," he said aloud.

He heard a groan and looked to his left on the steps. It was Agent Banks. Flynn gently shook her to wake her up.

"Where am I?" she asked, her eyes still closed. She rolled to her left and nearly tumbled down the steps before Flynn grabbed her.

Both eyes open and wide, she stared at Flynn.

"We're on the steps of the Bank of Olympia," he said.

"What the—"

"Yeah, my sentiments exactly."

She sat up and held her head in her hands. "I don't feel so good."

"Me either."

"Do you even remember what happened last night?"

Flynn shook his head. "I remember you collapsing right outside of the restaurant—and then it was like this strange dream. Some guy with a digitized voice droning on about something. I can't even remember what he was saying." He paused. "Maybe something about D.B. Cooper's twin. I don't know."

"Okay, that either wasn't a dream—or that's very odd—because I had the same one."

"Did you recognize the guy?"

"Nope. Never seen him before—and I definitely won't be able to recognize him by his voice either."

"Somebody is just toying with us."

Banks remained hunched over. "Oh, my head."

As she was moaning, a man draped a blanket over her head.

"Hey!" she said, tossing the blanket aside and looking up at the man.

"If you homeless people are going to sleep on the steps, I suggest you either remove yourselves by the time the sun comes up or take refuge in the shelter right down the street. Otherwise, I might have to call the authorities."

"Watch your attitude there, mister," Banks growled. "We are the authorities."

The man laughed and stepped over her as he ascended the stairs. "That's a good one." He turned around. "I'm going into my office. If you're not gone in five minutes, I'm going to have the Seattle PD remove you."

Banks dug in her pocket and held up her badge. "I'd like to see them try. Agent Banks, FBI."

"So grumpy in the morning. If that's an authentic badge of an FBI agent, I might inquire as to where you got it."

"Quantico. Any more questions, wise guy?"

"No, but I do have a bit of advice. If this was a stake-out of sorts, you might consider being more discreet. Your attire is a dead giveaway."

She stood up. "So, which is it? We look homeless or we look like federal agents—because it's not both."

He nodded at her. "Good day." He turned and walked up the steps before disappearing inside the building.

Neither of them moved from their spot. They were still in mild shock over the fact that they woke up outside and had very little recollection of the night before.

Banks picked up her phone and called Jones.

"Where are you?" Jones asked. "Thurston's been looking for you all morning and you weren't answering your phone."

She pulled her phone away from her ear and noticed the ringer was silenced. "Tell him I'm sorry I'm late, but someone drugged me and Flynn last night at dinner and dumped us on the steps of the Bank of Olympia downtown."

"Bloody hell, Banks," Jones said. "Are you okay?"

"I'm fine other than a sore neck and back. Think you can come get us."

"Sure thing. We're going to nail this bastard."

"I second that."

"Hold tight. I'll be right there."

Banks ended the call. "Jones is on his way to pick us up."

Flynn nodded. "Heckuva first date, eh?"

She smiled and shook her head. "Is that what this was?"

He shrugged. "Well, it certainly turned out to be more than two friends just having dinner."

"I do have to give you an A for originality. I can honestly say I've never been on a first date that involved getting drugged, kidnapped, and dumped outside to sleep it off."

"I like to think outside the box."

She smiled and then a serious look swept across her face. "So, do you think someone is trying to tell us something?"

"What do you mean?"

"I mean, was someone trying to point us in the right direction—or scare us?"

Flynn sighed. "This felt more like the work of a deranged criminal as opposed to someone trying to give us a clue as to who is behind the robbery. If you have a clue, why not just tell us? Why go through this grand production?"

She nodded. "Yes, and why stalk us to the restaurant?"

"That's an even better question—and has an answer that makes me very uneasy."

"Like someone is watching us?"

"Not just *someone*, but the very person we're hunting."

She scanned the street below. "Well, the sky diving shop owner did say the man had a connection to the Bank of Olympia."

"Surely, he wouldn't bring us here."

"It's pretty brazen, but how else would you explain us winding up here this morning?"

"Unless the suspect wants to get caught. Perhaps he

wants all the glory that D.B. Cooper never got to experience." He shook his head. "All these years later, and we still don't know Cooper's real name."

"If what you're saying is true, this guy is a real megalomaniac."

A loud shout caught Flynn's attention. "Speaking of megalomaniacs—"

"I thought I told you two to vacate the premises," the man from the bank said. "Or perhaps I wasn't clear enough the first time around."

Banks whipped out her badge. "Perhaps I wasn't clear enough either. Someone dumped us here last night and we're trying to piece together what we can from the scene. So, take your street sweeper act somewhere else because we're not moving until we're done here. Comprende?"

The man seethed as his eyes narrowed. He descended the steps until he was one step above Banks. "I'll have you know, Agent Banks, that I know your director."

"Congratulations. So does my mother. Now leave us alone before I start digging into your personal life and unearthing all your skeletons, Mr.—"

"Gordon. Carlton Gordon. And don't you forget it. It's a powerful name in the city."

"Names don't scare me, Mr. Gordon. But I suggest if you want to keep your name held in high regard, you let the people trying to keep this country safe do their job."

Gordon spun around and walked away without another word. He was almost at the top step when a man on the street shouting his name made his freeze.

Flynn glanced down at the street and smiled as he shook his head.

"Carlton Gordon, I need to have a word with you," a man on the street yelled.

Flynn knew that voice, the voice of none other than Harold Coleman.

Gordon turned his back and headed for the door.

"I'm onto you, Mr. Gordon. I know who you are."

# CHAPTER 19

COLEMAN SHIELDED HIS EYES as he looked up the steps toward the glass building reflecting the sunlight. He glared at Gordon.

"Don't walk away from me," Coleman shouted.

Gordon spun and galloped down the steps toward him. He stopped halfway down the steps, right in front of Flynn and Banks.

"If all three of you don't leave in one minute, I am going to call the police and have you forcibly removed. This is a respectable place of business." He then scurried up the steps and disappeared inside the building.

Coleman hustled up to Flynn and Banks as quickly as his cane would take him. "The man you're looking for just went inside that bank. What are you still doing standing here?"

Banks eyed him closely. "Let me get this straight. *That's* the guy who jumped out of the airplane and stole all the money?"

"That's exactly what I'm saying."

"I just can't go arrest a guy without reasonable cause— surely you haven't been gone from the Bureau that long that you've forgotten how things are done."

"No, I haven't forgotten, but I'm telling you right now, that's him."

Banks nodded. "Okay, I'll look into it. It seems quite odd given my experience over the past twelve hours, but I promise I'll do my due diligence."

"Good," Coleman said. "You won't be sorry." He traipsed up the steps.

"Hey, Agent Coleman. Where are you going?" Banks said.

He stopped and turned toward them. "You might be done, but I'm not. I've got a few more questions for him."

On the street a car beeped its horn and the driver gestured toward Banks and Flynn to get in.

"Don't do anything you'll regret," Banks called over her shoulder at Coleman.

Coleman smiled and opened the door.

*I can promise you I won't regret a single minute of this.*

With surprising agility, Coleman tapped his way across the bank's marble floors and toward Gordon, who was engaged in a conversation with a young woman.

"Excuse us, Miss," Coleman said. "I need to have a word with Mr. Gordon here, right now." He didn't wait for her to comply, nudging his way between them.

"I'm not going to ask you to leave again, whoever you are," Gordon said.

"Don't act like you don't know who I am," Coleman said, stamping his foot on his good leg. "Anyone who has gone through the painstaking detail to plot out a crime to, in my opinion, poorly replicate D.B. Cooper's skyjacking knows exactly who I am."

"I assure you that you're wrong, nor do I have any clue what you're insinuating."

Coleman edged closer. "I'm not insinuating a damn

thing—I'm telling you straight up: You were behind the recent heist."

"Mr.—" Gordon began.

"Coleman. Agent Harold Coleman."

"Mr. Coleman, I read about that. And while I hardly feel the need to dignify your accusation with a response, I will tell you that while the crime occurred, I was playing polo at the Ridgeline Golf and Polo Club. Anyone there that afternoon can vouch for my presence. Now, I'm not sure where you concocted such a hair-brained idea, but I suggest you keep it to yourself and exit the building before I make an even bigger scene and have security cart off a crazy old man."

Coleman bristled at his response. "I'm not buying your lies for one minute."

A smile spread across Gordon's face. "Well, *Agent* Coleman, why don't you do what you should've done the first time you had such a case land on your desk—and this time help the current authorities find the real criminal behind everything."

Coleman wagged his finger in Gordon's face. "We're not finished, you and me."

"I think we are," Gordon said, nodding in the direction of two security guards who'd been watching the entire scene unfold.

Coleman shrugged off one of the guards who grabbed his arm and limped toward the door. "I'm going. I'm going."

*But I'm not through with you.*

.

# CHAPTER 20

GORDON WEDGED HIMSELF into the aft cargo hold once again and waited for the plane to begin moving. As the jet engines fired up, a wry smile spread across his face. He was going to one-up D.B. Cooper.

He took a deep breath and relished the thought. His first attempt was about experiencing almost everything as Cooper did when it came to the jump—the weight of the money, the carefully planned escape route, the ability to remain anonymous. But this time, it was about nothing more than showing he could do it again. Even with ramped up security, he succeeded, even though it was considerably more difficult.

As he closed his eyes and braced for takeoff, he wondered what criticisms he would encounter this time. He loathed the fact that some people took issue with his facsimile of Cooper's original crime. The "#WannabeCooper" hashtag trended on Twitter and made him wince. In this day and age, such a skyjacking attempt would be impossible. No one could walk onto a plane with a bomb, or even pack it in their suitcase for that matter. It'd be too dangerous of a venture to have someone on the inside plant the bomb inside the cargo hold. About the only way to get a bomb past security and onto the plane would be to carefully bring the parts with you to work and build it on site—and even then there were a hundred things that could go wrong. So this was the next closest thing, a crime meticulously planned by Gordon, naysayers be damned.

With a little more scrutiny on him, Gordon exercised more caution this time in executing his plan. He wore a disguise that made him appear balding, just like that of Felicia's serious boyfriend, Steve Milton, who was slightly overweight as well, wore glasses, and appeared sloppy. Gordon served as a flight attendant on a corporate jet flight for a private airline one of his friends flew. With plenty of empty seats and an especially ornery group of passengers, the pilot received no pushback from management for creatively getting Gordon from Seattle to San Francisco on one of their planes.

Once in San Francisco, Gordon went to Felicia's apartment and surprised his "girlfriend." When she asked why he was home so early, he told her to get on something sexy in the bathroom, while he got ready. It was nothing more than a ploy to sneak into her purse and steal her access card—again. However, the plan nearly fell apart when Milton barged into her condo using the basement access. Thinking quickly, Gordon overwhelmed Milton from behind, putting him in a sleeper hold. He dragged his body downstairs without Milton ever knowing what hit him. In a matter of minutes, he was down the street and around the corner, feeding Doc a new set of Raleigh cigarettes.

"I never thought I'd see you again," Doc said, laughing at the irony of his statement.

Gordon said nothing.

"Well, go on. It's okay to laugh at my joke. I'm the one

blind. If I'm laughing, you should be laughing too."

Gordon chuckled and collected the last cigarette.

"Thanks, Doc."

"Why weren't you chatty this time?"

Gordon was already a few yards down the sidewalk before he responded. "Sorry, Doc. Maybe next time. I'm in a hurry."

That was ninety minutes ago—just enough time for him to get through security and sneak into the aft cargo hold before it was sealed for the flight.

The plane rumbled down the runway before the nose tilted upward and the plane lurched into the air.

A couple of hours later, Gordon opened the cargo door and fell from the sky under the cover of darkness. He deployed his parachute and barely made a mark when he hit the ground.

*A few more landings like that and I ought to become an instructor.*

He contemplated duplicating everything again but decided against it. Without any variety, the feds would know they were dealing with the same person. He at least wanted to seed the idea that they were dealing with the copycat of a copycat. It's why he wore a pair of shoes two sizes larger than he did last time. And instead of burying his chute, he took it with him, discarding it in a commercial dumpster behind a gas station a few miles down the road. He also maintained his disguise, one that would allow him to go virtually undetected if they were smart enough to suspect him. But he doubted they would.

Only that pesky former FBI agent continued to believe it was him.

*No wonder you never caught the original D.B. Cooper.*

He ditched his disguise in a public restroom near Pike Place Market on his way home. He donned a less discreet disguise for his reentry into his apartment.

Right before going to bed, he turned on his computer and looked at the front page of several national news websites.

## Cooper Copycat Strikes Again?

He smiled and turned his computer off before getting into bed. Now he experienced something Cooper never had: pulling off the same crime twice without getting caught—yet.

# CHAPTER 21

STARTLED AWAKE BY HIS ringing phone, Flynn rolled and grunted as he picked it up. Theresa Thompson's name flashed on the screen. For a moment, he contemplated throwing his phone across the room before answering it.

"Can't a man get a morning off to sleep?" Flynn grumbled.

"Not when the Cooper Copycat is stealing more money from the sky," she shot back.

"What?"

"You heard me. He struck again last night, this time stealing two hundred thousand on the exact same route from San Francisco to Seattle."

Flynn said nothing as he tried to process the news.

"Flynn? You still there?"

"Yeah, yeah. I'm trying to figure out what kind of criminal acts so brazenly." A pause. "And how did the San Francisco airport let this happen again? This is beyond believable."

"Well, believe it. And quit wasting time talking to me. You need to connect up with your FBI friends there and find out some more details. The wire reports were sketchy—and as you know, our readers will be looking for more from us, especially from you."

"I'm on it. I'll keep you posted."

Flynn rolled out of bed and stretched. He looked at his watch. He preferred not to get up before at least nine o'-clock on Saturday mornings, but duty beckoned. And as disappointed as he was about losing sleep on the weekend, he tried to stay positive.

*At least I didn't spend last night outside on the steps of a bank building.*

Yes, there was that.

He showered quickly before calling Banks.

"What's this about another Cooper Copycat heist?" he said once she answered her phone.

"Yeah, I didn't want to drag you into this after what we went through the night before."

"Seriously?" Flynn shook his head. "I live for this stuff, you know that."

"I know, but in my defense, I was alerted to this at four-thirty in the morning. I doubted you'd want to get *that* call."

"You're probably right. Can you bring me up to speed?"

"Get on out to Nisqually and I'll tell you all about it."

"He landed there again?"

"Yeah. He's taking this copycat thing to a whole different level."

"He's copying himself now?"

"Maybe."

Flynn pulled on his pants, while trying to hold his phone against his ear with his shoulder. "What do you mean, maybe?"

"We're not sure yet, but it could be someone copying the copycat."

"You've gotta be kidding me?"

"I wish I was, but I'm not—and this case just got that much more interesting."

"Okay. I'll be down there shortly, bearing gifts."

\*\*\*

FLYNN SAUNTERED UP TO THE SITE at Nisqually where a forensics team was going through the same protocols that helped them unearth other clues about the case just days before. He handed a cup of coffee to Banks and Jones. They both thanked him but didn't get a chance to say anything more than that when one of the forensics team members piped up.

"Perhaps we should petition to have the Bureau build us a field office on site," he said.

"Or you could just paint a big bull's-eye out here for him to land in, maybe keep all the evidence in one centralized location?" Flynn quipped.

Banks tried to stifle a laugh while swallowing her coffee.

"Can't you at least let me drink this in peace?" Banks said.

Flynn chuckled. "I brought my gifts—and a little humor for your Saturday morning." He paused and looked around. "Apparently, you're the only one who thought that was funny."

She leaned in to him and spoke softly near his ear. "I don't think that guy was kidding. He actually is suggesting we put this in the budget as a line item for next year. He's mentioned it three times now."

Flynn nodded. "I see."

"So, I'm sure you want the scoop, right?"

"Give it to me straight."

She took another sip of her coffee. "Okay, here's what we know. He jumped out of a plane in the exact same location as Saturday. However, he only stole $200,000."

"A tip of the hat to D.B. Cooper, no doubt."

"Maybe. Or maybe he didn't want all that extra weight." She paused. "I'm just spitballing here, but maybe it is another person."

"What would make you think that?"

Banks had a mouthful of coffee, so Jones jumped in. "Shoe size. This time the tracks we found correlate with what we believe to be a jumper landing were two shoe sizes bigger."

"Maybe that was to throw us off the trail?"

Banks nodded. "Possibly. However, he also left eight Raleigh cigarette butts behind like last time. And if that's a copycat of the copycat, that's pretty impressive. I mean, who has cartons of Raleighs just sitting around? That brand has been defunct for years now."

Flynn shrugged. "There are a lot of people obsessed with Cooper."

"True, but that's a coincidence that's difficult to overlook. How could anyone plan a repeat crime so quickly?"

"You sound torn."

Banks nodded. "I am. I can't make heads or tails of this mess. At best, I feel like he's playing with us by dropping clues to throw us off track. At worst, we've got two separate criminals we're chasing."

"What about you, Jones? What do you think?" Flynn asked.

Jones shrugged. "It's hard to say at this point. I'm leaning toward it being a second copycat, but we still need to process more information."

Their conversation was interrupted by one of the forensic team members. "Agent Banks, I think we have something."

The trio walked over to him, but Banks did all the talking.

"What is it?" Banks asked.

"It's a hair. It's not much, but it's something."

"Run it through the database and see if it reveals anything."

He nodded. "At least this might help you rule out someone."

"Or rule them in."

Flynn smiled. "You're going to figure this out. Just hang in there."

She nodded. "We need a big break like this."

"You're not kidding," Jones added.

Their conversation was interrupted by a commotion about a hundred yards away. They all turned and looked toward the park entrance where several FBI agents were doing their best to restrain a man from breaking through the perimeter they'd set.

"Is that who I think it is?" she asked.

Flynn nodded. "He's unbelievable."

She looked at Jones. "Stay here with these guys. I'll handle this." She turned and started walking with Flynn toward the former agent who was fast becoming a nuisance. "Harold Coleman, when are you going to leave me alone," she muttered under her breath.

# CHAPTER 22

COLEMAN PLEADED WITH BANKS using his eyes. His words had done little to engender camaraderie thus far, so he decided to switch tactics and use good old-fashioned humanity.

"What is this all about?" Banks asked as she put her hands on her hips. "This is getting really old, *Harold*."

"I tried to stop him, Agent Banks, but he wouldn't listen," the FBI agent detaining him said.

"Let him go. He's harmless—or at least I'll make sure he stays that way."

The agent released him and returned to his post on the perimeter.

"Thanks you, Agent Banks," Coleman said. "Good to see you again—and you, too, Mr. Flynn."

"Enough with the pleasantries," she said. "What are you doing out here poking around my crime scene again?"

"I've got it all figured out. Carlton Gordon is your Cooper Copycat—and I can prove it."

She sighed and rolled her eyes. "How is this any different than what you said this morning, where you accosted him on the steps of his bank? Quite frankly, I'm surprised that he didn't have you arrested and press charges against you."

"Perhaps I was a bit too pushy this morning, but I know for a fact that it's him."

Flynn folded his arms and leaned in. "Go on."

"Whoever did this is someone who belongs to the Ridgeline Golf and Polo Club—and he's likely the same person who shot at you when you went out there to question a few people."

Banks shook her head. "We sent some agents back and they didn't find a thing. Not a shell casing. Not an eyewitness. Nobody saw anything."

"Of course, they didn't," Coleman said. "This guy is meticulous. He's covering his tracks."

Flynn eyed him carefully. "What makes you so sure that it was somebody from the club? There hasn't been any evidence to suggest as much."

Coleman paused. "Well—actually—"

"Out with it, Harold," Banks said. "Okay, so right after the news of this broke and then Thurston told me I couldn't get involved in any official capacity—"

"I think he told you to let the FBI handle it," Banks snapped.

"Yes, something like that. Well, anyway, I went out to the airport and was able to get access to the crime scene."

Banks rolled her eyes. "My blood is starting to boil." She folded her arms. "Who gave you access to the site?"

"I have friends," he said.

"And you probably told a few lies as well, didn't you?" Flynn said.

Coleman bobbed his head back and forth. "One man's lie is another man's truth."

"How did you even gain access to the site?"

Coleman winced as he answered her. "I may have over exaggerated my position as a consultant on the case."

"What kind of exaggeration? The kind that says 'I'm working as a consultant' when you really aren't? That kind of exaggeration?" she asked.

"I'm gonna plead the fifth on that line of question."

"Harold!"

"Okay, okay. It may have gone something along those lines."

Flynn didn't have the same amount of reason to be upset, interested only in one thing. "So, what'd you find?"

"This," he said, holding up a golf ball marker with the Ridgeline Golf and Polo Club crest on it.

"Where did you get that?"

"From the aft cargo hold on the plane," he said.

Flynn shrugged. "It could've fallen out of someone's golf bag."

Coleman shook his head. "Really? That's all you've got, Mr. Flynn. I've been watching you on television and reading your books for several years now, and you strike me as a far more imaginative person than that."

"Sometimes the easiest explanation is the correct explanation," Flynn said.

"There's nothing easy about finding a random golf ball marker from a club where one of the prime suspects is a member."

Banks took a deep breath. "I will admit that Mr. Gordon seems like a viable suspect at this point, but if there's one thing you need to know about the new age FBI, it's this: If we don't have enough evidence to convict, we don't arrest anyone. And even if Mr. Gordon is our man, we're still a long way from being able to amass enough evidence against him." She paused and glared at him. "Especially when some retired agent starts stomping around my crime scene and stealing evidence. I have half a mind to have you arrested and thrown in prison right now."

"Stick with your other half then," Coleman quipped. "If you want to catch this guy, you need to listen to me."

Her eyes widened. "I prefer to follow the evidence—but since you dabbled with the evidence, making it inadmissible, you've placed me in a difficult situation."

"Look, I'm sorry about that—I am, really," Coleman said. "But Thurston was playing Bureau politics when he didn't bring me on to consult. Nobody knows this case better than I do."

"Well, you should've nabbed Cooper when you had a badge. But now, after all that, here you are traipsing into another one of my crime scenes. Are you going to muck this one up, too?"

Coleman tapped his cane on a rock several times. "Would you calm down, Agent Banks? I've got something else you might want to look into."

She put her hands on her head and closed her eyes. "For God's sake, please tell me that you're not about to pull another piece of evidence out of your pocket."

"No, no more evidence—but a hunch."

She sighed. "I don't know how much more of this I can take."

Flynn smiled. "Just hear him out."

"Fine, go ahead," she said. "Let's just get this over with."

"The copycat—or as I like to call him, Gordon—has to have an accomplice somewhere in San Francisco, likely someone who works at the airport. There's no way he's getting such unfettered access to secure areas without some help."

"And what makes you think that?" Banks asked.

"It's a gut instinct."

"The same instinct that helped you the first time you had this case?"

"Don't be so catty," Coleman said. "If I were you, I'd start asking around in San Francisco."

"Thank you for your time, Mr. Coleman," she said. "Now please vacate the crime scene or I'll have you escorted away."

"I'm leaving, I'm leaving."

She watched him shuffle off.

"You don't have to be so hard on the old man," Flynn said.

"Were you here for the entire conversation? Or did you miss the part where he revealed that he violated the integrity of the crime scene without authorization—and then withheld the evidence from us?"

"Well, that's not entirely true. He did just give us the evidence; so technically, it hasn't been withheld. Perhaps you should take up your beef with the forensics techs who missed that evidence themselves and then proceeded to let Coleman snoop around unsupervised."

"Oh, you bet someone is going to be hearing about this."

"But you still have to do something with that information that Coleman gave you."

She cocked her head to one side. "Before I can do anything, let's talk with Gordon. I see plenty of circumstantial evidence, but nothing definitive yet."

"Maybe that hair sample will offer us a clearer picture of who's involved."

"Exactly. But in the meantime, we've got a suspect to question."

# CHAPTER 23

GORDON COUNTED THE STACKS of money and locked it away in his safe on Saturday morning. The night before he'd been so tired from his jump that he decided it was a chore that could wait. The process of logging all the money the first time was so tedious that he decided a sign of respect toward Cooper would be to take only $200,000. He had already experienced what it was like to jump out of an airplane with the weight of twenty-two pounds of paper money strapped to him, so why not jump with just $200,000?

He fixed himself a pot of coffee and then fired up his laptop to read about his triumphant heist. Early reports were that the FBI wasn't sure if it was the same copycat that struck on Saturday or if it was a copycat of a copycat.

"Yeah, like anyone else is smart enough to pull off a stunt like this," Gordon said aloud before taking another sip of his coffee.

Since he laid the groundwork ahead of time for two jumps, pulling it off was even easier the second time. He had anticipated the new protocols and procedures in place at the airport, so his plan to hide a second disguise when he first gained access proved to be a stroke of genius.

Editorial writers for both the Seattle and San Francisco

papers wanted to know how this could happen once, let alone twice.

"What if it was a terrorist who wanted to sneak a bomb onto the plane and kill everyone on board?" one writer opined. "It's obvious after this happening twice in one week that something is broken with the TSA's current system."

Gordon chuckled. "You bet there's something wrong—it's called a huge inconvenience."

He found another article where the writer was calling for the head of the TSA director.

"Like he's the one manning the security stations," Gordon said. "These people are clueless."

Then he started to read an in-depth story that included a timeline of the events as the feds had given them to the press. At the bottom of the article was his favorite picture meme where Michael Jackson is staring at a movie screen, eyes wide, with a carton of popcorn in his hand, saying, "I'm just here for the comments." And then he started to read the comments.

*"Who does this guy think he is? D.B. Cooper? What a cheap knockoff?"* wrote "The Real D.B." from Sausalito.

*"So, now we have a knock off of a knock off? It's bad enough that China clones our superior products, now they're knocking off our criminals,"* wrote Maude from Montgomery.

Gordon snickered. "Maude hasn't had her coffee this morning yet—or she's still drunk from last night because that makes no sense. Who said anything about the Chinese here?"

He read another one.

*"I hope they catch this guy and throw him in jail. What a gutless punk?"*

And another one.

*"At least the original D.B. Cooper had class. This guy is just a straight up thief."*

And again.

*"I remember when Cooper hijacked that plane many years ago. Everybody hated the government then and Cooper stood for the fight against the big government encroaching upon the little man. Not much has changed since then. Everybody hates the government—and it's still encroaching on the little man. But at least we're not celebrating a criminal this time around."*

Gordon yelled at his screen. "Oh, come on, man. Where's the love?"

He quickly discovered there was no love for his crime spree. In fact, it was mostly disgust and hate.

Hoping for a better outcome on social media, he checked all the major sites—Facebook, Twitter, Instagram. The hashtag "#NotTheRealCooper" was trending everywhere, used as an addendum to cheap knockoffs. It seemed to be a sentiment that was picking up steam online.

"What is wrong with you people?" Gordon said, throwing his hands up in the air. "I'm not the villain here. Our greedy government is the enemy in this story."

Not that Gordon believed what he was saying. He didn't care what the government did—and his actions certainly had nothing to do with a principled stand. And he knew it. But when he complained out loud, it made him feel better, like he was more than a common thief. Because he wasn't a common thief. He was an exceptional one, one who had just stolen $1.2 million from the federal government and nobody seemed to be the wiser.

Well, almost nobody.

"I just don't get this," Gordon said. "People should be chanting my name in the streets instead of making derisive comments on social media toward me. Some people." He sighed and shook his head.

He was about to turn his computer off when an article headline caught his eye.

### Why America Loved D.B. Cooper
### (and Why It Hates His Copycat)

Gordon clicked on the link and it took him to *The International's* website for an article written by none other than James Flynn.

"This ought to be good," Gordon said to himself as he took another swig of his coffee.

The article started off by explaining what Gordon already knew—that the federal government's new regulations were starting to squeeze out many in the logging industry in 1971. People who once had well-paying jobs were now unemployed. To find work, they either had to uproot or take a job that paid far less. Environmental activists cared more about their cause than their fellow humans—and the fellow humans who were suffering the brunt of such policy decisions grew to resent the federal government's intrusion into their way of life. Bumper stickers cropped up with catchy phrases like, "Support environmentalists … with a rope," along with an image of a tree with a noose hanging from it. The movement to save the planet began in earnest with them losing their livelihood—and with nary a concern for how people in the field might adapt and provide for their families. The government had created expensive policies—and a new class of welfare recipients—in one fell swoop.

Ultimately, that's why D.B. Cooper was so popular, Flynn wrote. He was David against Goliath. He was taking a swing at the playground bully and getting the better of him. Everyone admitted what he did was a crime, but some people wondered if it was any less criminal than what the federal government was doing to them by taking away their jobs. He was the everyday man's hero.

And then there was the Cooper Copycat, who was universally despised by all. In the more than forty years since Cooper's heist, Americans have grown accustomed to the federal government's excessive regulation in all sectors of public commerce and private life. The idea of privacy was no longer a sacred right people held to. People realized their privacy was gone the minute they logged into Facebook or typed out a tweet on Twitter.

The Cooper Copycat couldn't generate sympathy from this America because it didn't view his heist as some worthy cause. Instead, it was just another entitled person trying to steal something from a more deserving citizen.

Gordon sighed. This wasn't how it was supposed to go. He was supposed to be the hero.

He closed his eyes and winced from the pain in his stomach. Moments later, he was experiencing another one of his coughing fits, the kind that resulted in him spitting blood into the sink.

Trying hard to put the pain aside, Gordon tried to come up with another plan. America loved a good comeback story. And while Mr. Flynn may have explained precisely why he wasn't as beloved as his criminal predecessor, no person was beyond redemption in the public eye. What celebrity hadn't been maligned by the general population at some point, and then praised again after a matter of time? The only ones who never recovered were those who made brazen political statements. And while he wasn't exactly a household name—yet—his crimes sure were. Every conspiracy theorist in the country was brushing up on their D.B. Cooper history whether they wanted to or not. The Cooper Copycat struck like lightning—now it was time to win over America's hearts and minds.

Gordon's phone buzzed. He looked at the caller ID and contemplated letting it go to voicemail. But he relented and answered after a few moments.

"What is it?" Gordon asked.

"Have you seen the news?"

"Of course, I have—it's ridiculous."

"Anything I can do to help at this point?"

Gordon sighed. "You've done enough already, but if you're feeling rather generous with your time, keep an eye out for me. There's a guy by the name of Harold Coleman who is beginning to cause some trouble. He's been poking around the crime scenes and is a former FBI agent. He's the former agent who was on the original Cooper case and never caught him. But he's crazy and determined. Think you can handle it?"

"I'll do my best."

Gordon hung up.

He stood up and grimaced. While he would rather stay in bed, there was no time for that. He had to give the public a show.

*They're gonna get a show they'll never forget.*

# CHAPTER 24

FLYNN TAGGED ALONG with Banks and Jones as they went to Gordon's downtown condominium. Banks felt certain nothing would come of Coleman's crazed ramblings, but unlike Coleman, she was going to be thorough. The last thing she wanted was the stigma of an agent who can't close a brazen case attached to her file.

Banks knocked on the door and waited for Gordon to answer.

A buzzer went off, followed by Gordon's voice. "Yes?"

"Mr. Gordon, I'm Agent Banks along with Agent Jones from the FBI. We have a few questions for you. It'll only take a minute of your time."

Several clicks and clunks later, the door swung open. "Won't you come in?" he said, gesturing for them to join him inside.

Banks went in first, followed by Jones. But when Flynn started to enter the condo, Gordon slid in front of him.

"And who are you?" Gordon asked.

"This is James Flynn," Banks said. "He's consulting with us on this case."

Gordon took a short step back. "Wait! *The* James Flynn? The conspiracy writer James Flynn? The former CIA operative who was banned for blowing the whistle on some shady government activity?"

Flynn smiled and nodded. "What government activity isn't shady?" Then he winked.

"I heard that, Flynn," Banks said from across the room.

"That's me. The one and only," Flynn said.

"Well, this is a surprise. You're one of my favorite authors. I have several of your books right here."

"Want me to sign one for you?"

Gordon's eyes lit up. "Would you? It'd be such an honor to have your autograph."

Flynn nodded. "Anything for my readers."

Gordon hustled across the room to grab a copy of Flynn's latest book, *Blood Treasure: The Truth behind the Nazi's Hidden Treasure Trove.* He handed it to Flynn and snagged a pen off his desk.

"I hate to break up this little fan boy moment, Mr. Gordon, but we didn't make this visit simply to arrange a meeting with your favorite author," Banks said.

"No, of course you didn't," Gordon said. "I think I know what this is about." Gordon gestured for them to sit down, and they complied. "I feel horrible about how I treated you yesterday and there's simply no excuse for it. I've decided to donate a large sum of money to the Seattle Area Homeless Shelter."

"Hopefully not $1.2 million," Jones said.

"I beg your pardon," Gordon said.

Banks scowled at Jones. "Actually, this isn't about yesterday either—well, at least not about Mr. Flynn and myself waking up on the steps of your bank like a pair of vagrants."

Gordon turned toward Flynn. "Was that you yesterday?"

Flynn smiled and nodded. "I'm afraid so."

"Oh, I'm doubly embarrassed now. I didn't even recognize you then."

Flynn took a deep breath. "It's okay. We looked like hell and had been through it, too."

"My goodness. What happened?"

Banks leaned forward from her seat on the couch directly across from Gordon. "We're not here to talk about *that* either."

"So what does bring you here today?" Gordon asked.

"This is routine for us, but we feel the need to rule out all suspects, even ones who have been accused by a former FBI agent."

Gordon closed his eyes and shook his head as if he were shivering. "Harold Coleman." He opened his eyes. "That man belongs in a psyche ward somewhere. He won't leave me alone."

Banks forced a smile. "Hopefully, your answer to this question will change all that."

"Fire away."

"Where were you on Saturday?"

"*This* Saturday?"

She nodded.

"Well, let's see. I left work early in the afternoon. Ate a late lunch at the Ridgeline Golf and Polo Club, played polo, came home and then went out to dinner."

"Did you dine alone or meet someone?"

"I ate by myself, but I can show you the receipt if you like."

"That'd be great."

After a few minutes of opening and shutting drawers in the kitchen, Gordon returned empty handed. "I seem to have misplaced it."

"Don't worry about it right now. How long did you play polo?"

"We quit right around five o'clock."

Banks stood up and offered her hand to Gordon. "Thank you for your time, Mr. Gordon."

"That's it?" he asked.

"We'll have to corroborate your story with people at the club," Jones said. "But based on your story, it would rule you out as a suspect."

Gordon laughed. "Just the idea that I would jump out of an airplane with thousands of dollars strapped to me is ridiculous. As you can see from my place, I do pretty well financially. What the Cooper Copycat took was pocket change for me."

"Again, just doing our due diligence, Mr. Gordon," Banks said.

"Once I'm ruled out, will you let Mr. Coleman know? Quite frankly I'm tired of being harassed by him and it's beginning to test my patience."

"I'll call him for you myself," Jones said.

"Fantastic. Thank you for stopping by—especially you, Mr. Flynn."

"I'm sorry it had to be under these circumstances," Flynn said. "Perhaps next time it won't be this way."

Gordon shook his hand. "Hopefully, it'll be *very* different."

Once they exited, no one said a word until they reached their car.

"What do you think?" Jones asked.

"I think we're all heading over to Ridgeline to check out his alibi before I draw any conclusions." She paused. "But something in my gut tells me he's lying."

Jones shook his head and laughed. "In your gut? You're starting to sound like Coleman."

Banks twisted the key in the ignition and her car roared to life. "Maybe Coleman's not as crazy as we think he is."

\*\*\*

THE SUN SAT JUST ABOVE the pines surrounding Ridgeline's grounds. Flynn swore if it ever snowed there, it'd be a dead ringer for a scene from the Swiss Alps. Banks' car bumped over the cobblestone driveway again, while Flynn stared intently at the polo game unfolding across the field.

Banks parked her car and left the door open for the valet, who rushed over with a claim check. The trio went inside and requested Henry Elberton. A few moments later, he arrived wearing a scowl on his face.

"What brings you back to Ridgeline, Agent Banks?" he asked, dispensing of any formalities.

"We need to ask around the polo grounds about a member of yours, a Mr. Carlton Gordon."

Elberton nodded. "Mr. Gordon is an exemplary member of the club and a sporting polo player."

"We're not here to inquire about his polo skills, but if he was here playing on Saturday."

"Indeed he was," Elberton said with a smile. "I play myself sometimes when a member can't make it, and we were teammates on Saturday."

Banks sighed. "If it's all the same to you, Mr. Elberton, I'd like to ask a few other players as well."

"Very well. Have it your way." He signaled for the attention of another attendant. "Would you take these three down to the polo field? It shouldn't take long."

"Thank you, Mr. Elberton. Have a nice day," Banks said before falling in line behind the attendant.

"That guy gives me the creeps," Jones said.

Flynn looked at him with an inquisitive look on his face. "You know him?"

Jones shook his head. "No, but just the way he acts is so smarmy and fake. It just makes me uneasy."

Banks turned around. "That's why we're going to talk to some other players," she said softly.

After a short walk, they arrived at the field and began milling around. "Let's split up," Banks said.

Following several minutes of questioning, they regrouped.

"What did you guys hear?" she asked.

"They all said the same as Elberton, basically," Flynn said. "That they were playing polo together until a little after five in the afternoon."

"Jones?" Banks said.

"Same here. And based on those people verifying his alibi, there's no way he could make it to San Francisco, slip through security, and jump out of a plane in less than six hours."

Banks nodded. "I agree. He's got to be ruled out as a suspect. Jones, let Harold Coleman know that his gut was wrong—and tell him to leave Gordon alone."

"You got it." He pulled out his phone and started dialing a number.

While Jones was doing that, Banks' phone rang.

"Agent Banks," she said as she answered.

"Yes, this is Alicia Armstrong with the FBI tip line. We just received a call that I wanted to let you know about immediately."

"Go on."

"One of the security operators at the San Francisco airport called to tell me that they found a work uniform of a Miss Felicia Davis stuffed in a trash bin. The operator checked with her employer to see if she'd been scheduled to work that day but didn't show up. She wasn't. And then here's where it gets crazy—the operator reviewed the security footage and found where Miss Davis apparently went into a family bathroom at the airport and changed. But only a man exited. The operator did some amateur sleuthing before he called the FBI and said it appears as though the man in the footage is also seen in pictures with Miss Davis on her social media sites."

"Thank you for passing this information along to me directly. Can you please forward it all to me in an email as well?"

"Will do."

Banks hung up and smiled as she looked at Flynn. "We might have just caught a big break in this case."

"Excellent," Flynn said. "Let's talk more about what this means in a moment. But first I need to use the restroom."

"I'll be here."

In the restroom, after Flynn had finished and was washing his hands, a young man approached him.

"Did I hear correctly that you were asking about Mr. Gordon?" the man said.

Flynn nodded. "And who are you?"

"I work here in the stables and watch all the polo games—and I have to say that Mr. Gordon looked a little off the last couple of times he's played."

Flynn furrowed his brow. "What do you mean by 'off'?"

"He wasn't playing like himself, like he'd almost never played the game before."

"But you saw him here on Saturday?"

The young man nodded.

"Unfortunately, we weren't here to rate his polo playing skills, just to verify if he was indeed present at the club on Saturday afternoon."

"If by present you mean physically here—yes, it looked like him. If by present in the context of a sound mind—no. He played like a rookie. And let me assure you that Mr. Gordon is no rookie. He's one of our better play-ers."

Flynn rubbed his chin. "I see."

"I just wanted to make sure you knew that, for what it's worth."

Flynn thanked him and exited the restroom.

***

AT THE SEATTLE FIELD OFFICE, Banks went alone into Thurston's office and closed the door.

"Did you see the email I forwarded to you?" she asked.

He nodded. "And what do you want me to do about it?"

"Authorize travel for me to go to San Francisco."

He sighed. "Come on, Banks. The San Francisco office

should be checking this out, not you."

"Yeah, but even so, I need to go there. I want to get a feel for how this seems to be happening with such ease at the airport."

He stood up and started to pace around his office. "You know DHS won't like this if you start snooping around the airport. We'll get mired in a territorial clash and lose valuable time and energy on finding the suspect."

"Finding the suspect? We haven't even identified him yet—and this is our best lead. You really want to turn this over to the San Francisco office or DHS, for that matter?"

"Fine. Make it seem like you're just going to their office to collaborate on the case. If they find out you were there but didn't connect with them, I'll definitely get my ass chewed out."

"Thanks. I don't think you'll regret this."

"And, Banks, leave Jones here with me. I've got a few other things I want him to run down."

"Can Flynn accompany me?"

"As long as its on his own dime." He paused. "And don't get too cozy with him. Journalists have a way of sticking around just long enough to get what they want and then leaving you high and dry."

She shook her head. "We're *way* past that point, sir. Just trust me, okay? He's proven to be a valuable asset on this case."

"Don't disappoint me, Banks."

She walked back to her desk where Flynn was waiting for her.

"Well?" Flynn said.

"Go grab a change of clothes. We're going to San Francisco."

\*\*\*

JONES DIDN'T LIKE THE FACT that Thurston let his partner head to San Francisco without him. It just didn't sit well with him for some reason. Something was going on.

"Jones, make yourself useful," Thurston said when he came out of his office and found Jones staring at a blank computer screen. "We're getting hundreds of calls each hour on the tip line. They're swamped. And while Banks is gone, I want you sorting through some of these. Maybe you'll get lucky and a credible tip will come directly to you."

Jones turned his back and rolled his eyes. "And I could win the lottery tomorrow as well."

"Then I guess it'd be a fine day all around if both those things happen." Thurston returned to his office, shooting Jones one more glance before he closed the door.

After sifting through note after note of tips that were less helpful and more like a waste of time, Jones' phone rang.

"Agent Jones."

"Yes, Agent Jones, this is Malinda from the tip line. I tried to reach Agent Banks but her phone goes straight to voicemail."

"We're working closely on this case. What's going on?"

"Well, I have a gentleman on the line who wants to speak with an agent directly and refuses to tell me anything. It could be nothing, but better safe than sorry, right?"

"Patch him through."

After a few clicks, Jones knew Malinda was no longer on the line.

"Hello?" Jones said.

"Yes, Agent—"

"Agent Jones."

"Okay, Agent Jones, I'm calling to tell you that I know who the Cooper Copycat is."

"And how's that?"

"I know him."

"And he confessed to you."

The man chuckled. "No, of course not. But I know it's him."

"Does this man have a name?"

"Yes, his name is Carlton Gordon. And I play polo with him. I've long suspected him as someone involved in corporate espionage for several reasons. First, no bank manager makes as much money as he appears to have. And second, I had patents stolen from safety deposit boxes there."

"Well, your suspicion of him alone doesn't make him a viable suspect."

"Exactly. I was only telling you that so I could tell you this—I hired a private investigator a few months back to follow him around. And when I got my weekly report today, I was surprised to see him track Mr. Gordon's movements to a private airfield at the same time he was playing polo with me."

"Perhaps your P.I. is fleecing you."

"I might think the same thing if not for the fact that I noticed something was strange about Gordon this past week when we were playing polo. His game was really off and he seemed to avoid talking to the other players, which isn't like him. Not every day, but on two specific days—last Saturday and this Friday. And those were the days the Cooper Copycat struck. Plus when I started to think about it some more, I realized he would actually be able to find out when the San

Francisco Federal Reserve office was sending money to his bank, probably because he ordered it."

"Well, Mr.—"

"Goodyear, Edwin Goodyear the Third."

"Okay, Mr. Goodyear. That sounds well and good, but it's not exactly an actionable tip."

"I'm telling you, he's your guy."

"Did your P.I. take pictures that were time stamped?"

Goodyear sighed. "No, he said his camera broke last week and he's still waiting for it to get fixed."

"There you go, Mr. Goodyear. Problem solved. You need to hire a different P.I. and replace the lazy one you've got."

"But I swear to you, that's what is going on."

"And you're not just saying this because you saw agents milling around Ridgeline this afternoon asking questions about Mr. Gordon?"

"I didn't even know about that, honest."

"We'll take your tip and look into it when we get a chance. Thank you for taking the time to reach out to the FBI."

"Don't dismiss me," Goodyear said. "I'm telling you the truth."

"Good-bye, Mr. Goodyear."

Jones hung up—and scratched out a few notes about the call before placing it on Banks' desk.

# CHAPTER 25

HAROLD COLEMAN PULLED his Washington Huskies sweatshirt over his head and grabbed his ticket off his dresser. After he graduated from Washington, he bought season tickets for all the football games. It turned into a fall tradition for the entire family. Once his children were old enough to get on a boat without diving into the water, he bought a sailboat so the family could "sailgate" before all the games. Those days were long gone now, as his children had grown up and moved away. And Edith preferred to churn through the pages of the latest mystery novel atop *The New York Times* best seller list on her free Saturday evenings.

But not Coleman. He was in the stands in 1975 when Warren Moon's pass was tipped and landed in the hands of receiver Spider Gaines for a stunning victory over Washington State. He was present in 1992 when the Huskies played Nebraska for the first night game in school history and pulled out a victory to propel the team to the top spot in the polls. He was also there in 2000 when Washington upset No. 4 Miami to ruin the Hurricanes' national title hopes. And nothing was going to keep him out of the stands for a Huskies' home game.

Well, almost nothing.

"Good-bye, beautiful," he said as he kissed Edith on top of the head.

She patted him on the shoulder and turned the page in her book. He was standing at the door when she finally looked up.

"Harold! What are you doing? Are you about to leave the house without your lucky hat?"

He smiled. "A senior moment," he said, shuffling back toward the closet and fetching his purple and gold baseball cap.

She eyed him closely. "I'm glad you can watch the game in peace tonight, dear."

"What do you mean?"

"Well, since the FBI cleared that banker guy you were so obsessed with you can move on."

"That doesn't exactly equate to peace for me. I'll have peace when the copycat is behind bars—and someone finds Cooper's remains in the mountains."

"Either way, have fun. And beat those Cougs!" she said.

Coleman chuckled to himself as he walked out the door and climbed into his car. He wanted to brood over her statement, even though he knew she was right. Agent Jones had called to tell him that they were removing Carlton Gordon from their suspect list. But he wasn't so sure. But it created the perfect opportunity for him tonight.

His thoughts shifted back toward his sweet wife, who acted like she didn't care about football yet still knew whom the Huskies were playing. Even several years ago when she decided she didn't want to attend all the games, she almost always went to the Apple Cup game when Washington squared off with their rivals, the Washington State Cougars. But then she grew tired of the fighting the crowds.

Coleman tossed his hat on the seat next to him and folded up his cane. He dialed his buddy's number to deliver the news.

"Oscar, just calling to let you know I'm not going to be at the game tonight," Coleman said.

"Are you in the hospital?"

"No, but I do have more pressing matters tonight."

"What could be more pressing than watching the Apple Cup?"

Coleman sighed. "There's more to life than football."

"Harold, I'm worried about you. Did you fall and hit your head?"

Coleman chuckled. "I'm fine. And I'll see you soon, don't you worry. Just don't let them lose tonight, okay?"

He turned off his phone and placed it in the cup holder next to him.

Coleman smiled as he pulled out of the driveway. It'd been a long time since he was on a stakeout.

\*\*\*

COLEMAN TURNED THE RADIO on to listen to the game. And while he knew a stakeout required great vigilance, it also required a strong distraction. When men tend to sit alone and think by themselves for too long, they lose touch with reality. They either start to think that the world's problems are easily solvable—or they conclude there is no hope. Partners often helped mitigate this dangerous death spiral of a man left to his thoughts, but Coleman preferred being alone tonight.

Truth be told, he would rather be sitting at Husky Stadium, doing his best to urge on his alma mater to victory with his feeble voice. But sometimes there are things a man just has to do.

Naturally, Coleman's thoughts drifted back to 1971 when he was still a young agent in every way possible. Not two years out of Quantico, he was working on a case that had gripped the nation. While he couldn't discuss the investigation with anyone, the fact that he was on it—and all his friends knew it—became a source of pride. That pride soured over time, turning into shame. Instead of his friends bragging to others at parties and pointing in his direction that they knew the guy trying to catch D.B. Cooper, they eventually began to ask him privately in hushed whispers, "When are you ever gonna catch that guy?"

After all these years, Coleman had to answer that question truthfully: Never. D.B. Cooper was gone forever. Conspiracy theorists presented him with plausible ideas as to who the criminal was and how he pulled off the skyjacking, but they all lacked one thing—the confession of a living person. Deathbed confessions held little weight for Coleman, especially pertaining to a case so old that it would be difficult to verify it. Over the years, he'd heard about so many of them that he stopped paying attention. Only one man knew the truth—and that man was Dan Cooper. Whoever he was, he'd pulled a fast one on the FBI and became a celebrated cultural icon in the process.

And now there was another man attempting to do the same thing, but with far less success. So far, he'd flummoxed the Bureau's pursuit. Coleman didn't want to see a second man celebrated for the same crime, even if the public's general feeling toward the criminal seemed to be more disdain than admiration.

He peered through his binoculars, following the shadows dancing in front of Gordon's window on the second floor of his condominium. So far, nothing.

As the night wore on, Coleman wondered if he'd become too obsessed with the case, to the point that he couldn't pick his way through this investigation. While he was no longer a paid professional, there was nothing amateur about what he was doing, except for the fact that he lacked the Bureau's funds and resources. Instead of a wiretap on Gordon, he had to sit outside and hope he went somewhere—someplace that would raise an eyebrow or two.

He looked at his clock. It was already nine o'clock and the second half of the game was about to kick off. Washington clung to a 17-14 lead, though he was convinced they'd blow it based on how the team's defense had been playing in the second half of its past few games.

He bit into an apple he'd brought. The sound of his teeth grinding up the moist fruit momentarily distracted him from the conversation playing in his head since he pulled out of his driveway.

Coleman was only three bites into his apple when he nearly dropped it.

*Tap! Tap! Tap!* Startled, Coleman glanced out his window to see an unexpected face.

"Edith! What in the world are you doing here?"

Her eyes narrowed. "I think that's a far more appropriate question for you than me."

"It's not what it looks like," he said.

"Oh, it's exactly what it looks like—and I'm here to help," she said, holding up a brown paper bag. "I've got some goodies inside—white chocolate macadamia nut cookies, your favorite."

He unlocked the door and she hustled around to the passenger side.

"Edith, I'm really—"

"Save your apology for someone who wants one," she said. "I knew you weren't about to give up so easily on this case."

"What gave it away?"

"I was suspicious when you didn't take your hat, because you never forget that. But it was Oscar's call at halftime that sealed it for me."

Coleman moaned. "Oscar, Oscar, Oscar."

"And it only took me two minutes to open your desk up and find an address written down with Carlton Gordon's name at the top, so I took a wild shot in the dark that I'd find you here. Plus, I've always wanted to go on a stakeout."

"You read too many mystery novels."

She smiled. "Perhaps I do, but here I am." She paused. "So, what do we do now?"

Coleman pulled his wife closer and kissed her on the forehead. "You keep me company. That's what you do."

She laughed. "And here I was having sympathy for you all these years for having to go on a stakeout. I had no idea it was this easy."

"Or boring. Just give it a couple of hours and you'll be wishing you were home reading another Karin Slaughter book."

"But until that moment comes—"

Coleman held up his hand. "Hush, honey. Look there. He's coming out of his condo."

She pressed her hands together and rubbed them. "Excellent. Now what do we do?"

Coleman fired up his engine and his lights flickered on.

He looked at her and flashed a toothy grin. "We're gonna go for a little ride."

# CHAPTER 26

GORDON LOOKED AROUND THE STREET and exhaled. For the first time in a few days, he could see life returning to normal again. His crime spree was fun, but he was done skydiving from airplanes and living in fear that at any moment the feds would charge into his condo and arrest him.

Despite being told he was no longer a suspect, Gordon suspected that wasn't really the case. He guessed that they were baiting him, telling him he was free so they could track his movements. The feds always assumed that guilty suspects will return to their wicked ways. And most of the time they were right. But not this time. Gordon was done living under the guise of suspicion. He was also done with sneaking around and planning every last detail to ensure he didn't get caught. It was an exhausting chore, one that required vigilance and diligence, a keen eye for details. Though he was confident he'd taken care of all the minutiae that often determine the difference between getting caught and getting away with it, he could never be a hundred percent certain. One overlooked detail could lead to his arrest.

Gordon adjusted his rearview mirror, trying to suppress the growing uneasiness he felt that someone was watching him. And that someone was a federal agent. But perhaps he was wrong—it wouldn't be the first time.

He concentrated on his driving, checking his mirrors periodically. Everything seemed fine for a while and fears unfounded, until it came time to make a turn onto a dirt road. He was going to visit a pilot, someone he'd have to persuade to take him up in the afternoon for a brief stint.

Then he looked again.

*Okay, I'm pretty sure that car is following me.*

He approached a private dirt road and turned the steering wheel violently to the right without the use of his blinker. The car behind him followed suit.

It only meant one of two things to Gordon. Either he was being followed or someone else was going to the same place he was. And neither one of those outcomes gave him much reason to be hopeful.

*Hang on, ladies and gentlemen. I'm about to show you how it's done.*

With that, Gordon jumped a small rise and then jerked his wheel hard to the right. In a matter of seconds he'd know if he was being tailed or simply being paranoid.

The car behind him still followed.

*Tailed!*

"I swear if that's Harold Coleman, I'm going to beat him to death and bury his dead body out here in the middle of nowhere," Gordon growled.

He jumped another rise and then saw his opportunity to shake him for good. Up ahead, the road narrowed to essentially one lane, thanks to a boulder that had tumbled off the side of the mountain a few years ago. If he slowed down enough to let the tail catch up with him, he could jerk his car to the left at the last moment and cause the car behind him to collide with the rock. It was the best idea he came up with on the spot.

As he slowed down, the car behind him sped up and nearly caught up to him. Gordon eased back onto the gas.

*Excellent!*

"In 3-2-1-" Gordon jerked the wheel at the last second to avoid the boulder. But the car behind him wasn't so lucky. The small rocks pinging around inside his wheel well as he hummed down the washboard dirt road were overwhelmed by the sound of metal colliding with rock—if only for a second.

Gordon smiled to himself and stopped his car. He wanted to admire his work. The air was filled with dust, smoke, and the hissing from a busted engine. The red glow of flashing hazard lights from behind the boulder indicated they'd survived, but they likely wouldn't be tailing him again, whoever they were.

As he walked back to his car, he felt a twinge in his stomach again. He tried to suppress the cough welling up in him, but he couldn't. More blood mixed with mucus spewed from his mouth and onto the dirt. He wiped his mouth with the back of his hand and climbed behind the wheel.

\*\*\*

FIVE MILES FARTHER DOWN the road, Gordon pulled into Northwest Aerial Services run by former crop duster Tommy Spurlock. Gordon knew about Spurlock's business from his bank. The Bank of Olympia had loaned Spurlock the money to buy a used Cessna 210 five years ago. And while Spurlock kept his account in good standing for the most part, he'd fallen behind for the past few months. His wife's sciatica reached a point that she could no longer function—or care for their four young children—if she didn't get surgery. And while they had insurance, the $12,000 deductible forced Spurlock to come up with a solution to pay for her surgery. His solution was to forego payments on his plane and beg for mercy. Oddly enough, he'd only received one call from the bank after ignoring the note for three months.

Gordon looked at Spurlock's file one last time and adjusted his fake goatee before knocking on the door.

The door creaked open with Spurlock standing there to greet him. He wore a pair of torn jeans and a faded Seahawks t-shirt.

"Can I help you, sir?"

Gordon took a deep breath and offered his hand. "As a matter of fact you can. My name is William McDonald, manager of the Bank of Olympia. I believe we have some business to discuss."

"Can't this wait? My wife is still laid up from surgery and I've got four little ones running wild right now who I need to get to bed."

Gordon stepped inside. "I'll wait." He hated lying to such a hard-working man living under tenuous circumstances, but he needed to coerce the man into helping him.

Spurlock sighed. He gestured toward the couch, covered in crumbs. "Have a seat and I'll be right back."

Gordon chose to investigate the haphazardly arranged family pictures on the wall as opposed to taking a seat on the couch and getting his butt covered in crumbled Doritos. With his head itching, he adjusted his scalp cap. After a few minutes of gazing at the Spurlock's family picture album plastered to the wall, Gordon resorted to surfing the web on his cell phone until Spurlock returned.

"I'm sorry about that, Mr. McDonald—I truly am," Spurlock said. "Can I get you something to drink?"

Gordon shook his head. "No, thank you. This won't take long."

Spurlock directed his guest toward his dining room table. "What's this all about?"

"I think you know."

Spurlock looked down and scratched at the table in front of him. "I've been trying to keep up with my payments—I really have. But when Linda got sick, I didn't know what to do. Business has been slow lately—and I just had to choose between paying the mortgage note on the plane and feeding my kids."

"I understand," Gordon said. "Surely you also must understand that our employees have kids to feed as well. And whenever someone defaults on a loan, we lose money—money we could use to pay our employees more fair wages."

"Look, I'm sorry. I really am." He paused. "Does this mean you're going to take my plane away from me?"

Gordon opened the folder and flipped through it, glancing at the papers inside. "I don't believe in kicking a man when he's down—but I do believe in a level of personal responsibility. You're responsible for this payment every month and you need to find a way to make sure this isn't late again. However, I can issue you a reprieve."

Relieved, Spurlock let out a long breath. "Thank you, Mr. McDoanld. I'll figure out something moving forward. Is there anything I can do for you?"

Gordon nodded and pushed his glasses up on his nose. "As a matter of fact there is. What's your flight schedule look like tomorrow?"

"Even if it was full, I'd clear it for you," Spurlock said with a smile.

"That's what I like to hear. I've got a very special assignment for you tomorrow."

# CHAPTER 27

BANKS RAPPED ON THE SCREEN DOOR of the apartment belonging to Felicia Davis. She turned her back to the door and closed her eyes, letting the Sunday morning sun warm her face and offset the brisk San Francisco breeze.

"This is not how I'd want to start my Sunday morning," Flynn said.

"Based on how long it's taking her to answer the door, my knock may have indeed started it."

After a few more moments, clinking of bottles and heavy footsteps could be heard coming from inside.

"Somebody's movin' around in there," Banks said.

"I don't want any," a woman's voice yelled followed by a prolonged coughing fit.

"Miss Davis, my name is Agent Banks with the FBI, and I have a few questions for you."

Flynn chuckled at the string of expletives Davis ripped off while walking toward the door.

"Just a minute," she said.

When the door swung open, Flynn and Banks were greeted by a woman who appeared to have rolled out of bed only minutes before. With frizzy hair, Davis wore a fuzzy pink bathrobe and had a cigarette hanging out of her mouth.

She leaned against the doorway on her left shoulder, refusing to open the screen door.

"What do you want?" Davis asked.

"We have a few questions for you, Miss Davis," Banks said as she held up her badge. "Mind if we come in?"

Davis opened the screen door and pointed toward the small table in the cramped apartment's kitchenette. "I'm gonna make some coffee so I can make some sense. Either of you want any?"

Banks and Flynn declined.

Davis tapped some ashes into the sink and took another long drag on her cigarette. "So, what'd Tim do this time?"

"Tim?" Banks asked.

"Yeah, my brother. I suppose this is about him, right? He's only been in and out of federal prison a half dozen times at least for robbing banks."

"Where does Tim live?" Flynn asked.

Davis shrugged. "Nebraska or Iowa—I don't know. Somewhere where they grow a lot of corn and he can distill his moonshine in peace."

"No, this isn't about Tim," Banks said.

Davis poured the water into the coffee pot. "Really? So, what's this fun little Sunday mornin' house call all about?"

Banks shook her head. "It's actually about you and—"

"Look, if this is about that bar fight last night, I didn't start anything. It just sort of happened. When that woman insulted my tattoo by calling it 'amateur hour,' I had to defend my honor. I know I hit her pretty hard. Is she okay?"

"I have no idea what you're talking about, Miss Davis."

Davis mimed zipping her lips. "I'll stop guessing and just let you tell me why you're here."

Banks forced a smile. "Thank you."

Davis slumped down into a chair at the table and tapped her cigarette on the edge of the ashtray located in the center of the table. She exhaled, blowing her smoke upward and away from her guests.

"Do you work at the airport, Miss Davis?" Banks asked.

She nodded. "Goin' on three years now, slingin' luggage for United."

"So, that's why my luggage always gets damaged when I fly United," Flynn said.

Davis snickered and shook her head. "Naw, that's just what we call it. We treat every bag with respect, as if it were our own."

Flynn glanced around at her apartment, quickly surmising that he and Davis had vastly different standards as it pertained to their personal belongings.

"I know this may sound like a silly question, but have you loaned your security badge to anyone lately?" Banks asked.

Davis laughed. "Lord, no. This is the most stable job I've had in ten years—I wouldn't do somethin' that stupid. Why do you ask?"

Banks leaned forward with her hands clasped. "It's the purpose for our visit, actually." She paused. "Have you heard anything about the Cooper Copycat case?"

"The guy who jumped out of a plane with a million

"That's the one."

"What about it?"

"We got a tip yesterday that whoever this was may have used your badge to access the security area."

Davis dismissed the statement with a wave. "That's crazy. I keep my badge with me at all times."

"Even when you're out on the town drinking?" Flynn chimed in.

She bristled at the question. "If it's not around my neck, it's in my purse—and nobody's touchin' my purse."

"What about any boyfriends?"

She laughed. "Honey, I ain't got a boyfriend smart enough to pull off a heist."

Banks folded her arms. "But you do have a boyfriend?"

"He's downstairs in the basement if you want to question him yourself. Just be forewarned—he's crazy."

Flynn flashed a quick smile at Banks. It's exactly what they wanted to do, though they never imagined they'd catch such a break with him being in the house.

Flynn and Banks followed Davis to the top of the basement stairs. Davis yelled down. "Get some pants on, Frank. We've got visitors."

"Geez, Felicia," came the response from below. Some heavy footfalls followed by a door slamming in the basement provided the soundtrack as they descended the steps.

Once they reached the bottom of the steps, a large man wearing an Oakland Raiders jersey and gray sweatpants with a large stain entered the room. He wiped his right hand on the side of his pants before offering it to the agents.

"Frank DeMillo," he said.

Flynn and Banks introduced themselves and took a seat on the couch at his behest.

"So, what do you guys wanna talk about?" DeMillo said.

Flynn pulled a picture out of his folder and held it up in front of DeMillo. "Is that you?"

DeMillo leaned forward and squinted at the picture. "Looks like me—definitely a handsome fellow."

Flynn withdrew and slid the photo back inside the folder.

"Mr. DeMillo, that picture is security footage from the San Francisco airport—and it coincides with the time that federal money was stolen by a parachuting thief," Banks said.

DeMillo snapped his fingers. "Yeah, I saw that. He's that Cooper Copycat, right?"

Banks nodded.

"Crazy, huh? That guy's got steel balls, I'll tell you that much. I've done some crazy stuff in my day, but jumpin' out of a commercial jet? Not my thing."

"So, who is this in the picture?" asked Davis, who wore a scowl on her face.

"I've got no idea, baby, but it ain't me."

Banks took a deep breath and exhaled before speaking. "Where were you on Friday evening, around seven o'clock?"

"I was teaching a class at my sky diving school," he said.

Flynn's eyes widened. "You're a sky diver instructor?"

"Yeah, I don't jump much any more—thyroid issue blew me up and landing is difficult on my knees. But I still teach a class. I got a dozen people who can vouch for me."

Banks bit her lip. "I'd like a roster because we're going

to need to check that out."

DeMillo shrugged. "Sure thing. It's crazy how much that guy looks like me, but it couldn't have been me."

"Do you have a twin?" Flynn asked.

DeMillo broke into a hearty laugh. "I'll tell you what my momma told me when I was growin' up. She used to say, 'Frank, when they made you, they broke the mold.' And I can tell you that there's only one person that looks like me, though I'm sure that comes as a disappointment to all the ladies out there." He looked at Banks and winked.

Banks pursed her lips and nodded slowly. "Okay, why don't you write down a list of the people in your class so we can follow up with them directly—and then we'll get out of your hair."

"You got it. Give me a minute." DeMillo stomped up the steps in search of pen and paper.

Flynn glanced back up the stairs to make sure DeMillo was out of earshot. "Now that Frank is gone, you want to tell us if there are any other people who might have been able to access your card and steal it."

"My card's never been stolen," she said. "I have it in my purse right here." She reached down on the table and started rifling through it. Nothing. "I know I have it here somewhere."

"Miss Davis, when was the last time you went to work?" Banks asked.

"I had surgery over a week ago on my back, but doc told me to avoid lifting heavy objects. That's how I got some free vacation."

"So, it's been over a week?"

Davis nodded.

Flynn held his gaze on her. "I don't think you answered my question. Were there any other people who perhaps had access to your badge?"

"I know I had it the other day," Davis mumbled, still digging in her purse. Then to Flynn, "I don't know if I understand what you're sayin'."

He sighed. "Let's see. How should I put this? Did you have a romantic rendezvous lately with someone other than Frank?"

She laughed. "All the time, honey. Frank and I have a very open relationship, if you know what I mean. It's the only way I can keep him, though he couldn't keep me satisfied if he tried."

Banks chuckled uncomfortably. "Did you have one of these encounters recently?"

Davis looked up and rolled her eyes around. "Let me think. There aren't many regulars, though I have a few who come into town and hit me up when they're lonely."

"Does the name Carlton Gordon ring a bell?" Flynn asked.

She shook her head. "Nope. Never heard of him."

He pulled a picture out of his pocket and held it up to her. "Still unfamiliar?"

She took it out of his hand and studied it closely, squinting as she scanned the photo. She then slowly shook her head. "Doesn't look like anybody I've ever seen."

"You sure about that?" Flynn asked.

"Yep. I'm sure," she said as she handed the picture back to him. "I have no idea who that guy is."

"Thank you for your time, Miss Davis," Banks said as they headed up the stairs. Once they reached the top, Banks handed Davis her card. "Give me a call if you think of anything else and update me on the status of your badge, one way or the other."

Davis took the card and nodded.

DeMillo wrote down the names and numbers of the people in his class and handed it to Banks once they reached the kitchen.

"Here you go," DeMillo said. "I even put my number on there in case you wanna follow up." He winked again.

Banks sighed. "Thank you both. Sorry to have troubled you."

Once they reached the sidewalk, Flynn didn't waste any time dissecting the questioning of the two strange characters.

"She's lying," he said. "No doubt about it."

"You think so?" Banks said. "She didn't seem like a liar to me."

"She had a few tells. When she was looking at that picture, the corner of her eyes flinched. She definitely had seen him before."

"What reason did she have not to talk then?"

"Embarrassment? Possible job loss? Hush money? Take your pick."

Banks nodded in agreement. "Yeah, there are plenty of reasons for her to remain quiet about any connection she might have to Gordon, if he indeed is our man. But she didn't know that."

"True, but why else would we be asking her about him? She had to know something was up, then."

"Maybe I can have the San Francisco office put a tail on her, watch her for a few days and see if she does anything strange."

"Good idea."

They continued along the sidewalk downhill until they reached the corner of 22nd and Capp Street, home to a small convenience store.

"Either of you have a cigarette I can bum off of ya?" came a man's voice.

Both Flynn and Banks turned around to see a man wearing dark sunglasses and clutching a walking stick. They exchanged befuddled glances.

"Yeah, you," the man said. "I may not be able to see you, but I know you're both there."

"Sorry, I don't smoke," Banks said. "But I'll get you a pack. What do you like?"

A wry smile spread across the face of the man. "If you can find me a pack of Raleighs, I'll be forever indebted to you. But since I doubt it, I'll settle for some Marlboro Ice Blasts."

"Never even heard of such a cigarette," she said.

The man chuckled. "Well, you're missing out, ma'am."

She went inside while Flynn remained outside to talk with the man.

"Did you say you like Raleighs?" Flynn asked.

The man nodded. "Best damn cigarette ever made."

"How'd you pick them?"

"Red Skelton introduced me to them on his radio show. I've never been much for television, if you catch my drift." He stopped to laugh at his own joke while Flynn joined him. "And then the coupons—got my first harmonica through Raleighs' redeemable coupons." He paused and shook his head. "Oh, the irony."

"Yeah, I'm thinking wind instruments and smoking don't mix well."

"True."

"So, do you ever get to smoke any Raleighs these days?"

The man rubbed his face with his right hand and turned his head in Flynn's direction. "Not very often, but I've run into some luck lately."

"Oh?"

"Yeah, some strange man popped by twice this week and just gave me Raleighs randomly."

Flynn studied the man intently. "What made him strange?"

"The fact that he collected all my cigarette butts. I mean, who does that? Me and that butt were intimate. It just kinda creeps me out."

"Are these your butts here on the ground?"

The man put both his hands on his hips. "Are you like this man, too? Is this some strange new fetish that I don't know about?"

"No fetish, just curious."

"Yeah, so I smoke a lot. Tell the environmentalists to stick it where the sun don't shine. I blow smoke often and I'm not ashamed of it."

Flynn stooped down and collected several butts. "So, when did this man come around?"

"Hmmm. I think maybe last weekend and just a couple of days ago. But don't quote me on that. He's been by here before, but never said anything."

"Not to be rude or anything, but how can you be sure?" Flynn asked.

"When you're blind, you learn to use your other senses—and that joker smells like he takes a bath in Stallion."

"Stallion?"

"Yeah, you never heard of it? It's a cologne for men. And quite frankly, you could use some."

Taken aback by the man's frankness, Flynn stood speechless for a moment.

"Didn't mean to offend you, mister. But I'm old and I'm blind—and I just tell it like it is."

"No offense taken," Flynn said. "So, does this strange man have a name?"

"I call him Mr. Money Bags. I don't really know much about him, but he smells like he bathes in Stallion and he works in a bank."

"Really? There's a scent for that?"

"The scent of money. It's unique—and undeniable. That's why I call him Mr. Money Bags. It certainly isn't for any bills he's pressing against my flesh," the man said as he pointed to the palm on his right hand.

Banks emerged from the convenience store with a pack of cigarettes in her hand, the cattle bell clanking against the door.

"Marlboro Ice Blast, just like you wanted," Banks said, handing the cigarettes to him. "Got you a new lighter, too."

"Your kindness knows no bounds, miss," the man said.

"You got a name?" Flynn said.

"Everybody calls me Doc," the man said. "I don't know why, but it stuck years ago."

"Well, Doc, I appreciate all your help," Flynn said.

"I didn't know you needed help," Doc shot back as he fired up a cigarette.

"We both needed it more than you know."

Flynn grabbed Banks by the arm and started across

the street.

"Wanna tell me what went on while you were out there talking with him?" Banks said.

"Your first big break in this case."

Banks shot him a confused look. "I'm not sure I follow?"

"I'll explain more later, but first let me ask you this: how well do you know your colognes?"

# CHAPTER 28

COLEMAN HANDED EDITH an icepack and sat down next to her on the couch. She groaned as she set the pack on her forehead, which sported a purplish bruise.

"If I hadn't told you to slow down last night, we might be in the hospital right now," she said.

Coleman nodded. "It definitely could've been worse. I'm just grateful it's not."

He shifted in his chair and looked at his wife, stroking the side of her face with the back of his hand.

"You've got to stop this, Harold," she said. "I mean, look at me."

"I never meant for you to get involved in any of this."

She cocked her head and narrowed her eyes. "I'm married to you. I'm always going to be involved in anything you do, whether I'm physically present with you or not." She paused. "What I think you meant to say was that you didn't mean for me to get hurt."

"No! I didn't mean for you to get hurt—in any way. Sometimes I get so driven—"

"Sometimes? *Sometimes*? Harold, I've been married to you for a long time and you can get driven about all sorts of things." She paused and held up her index finger for effect.

"But there's only *one thing* that gets you so driven that you're pushed to the brink of insanity. It's an unhealthy obsession."

He closed his eyes and leaned his head back on the couch, unsure of what to say next.

"You know I'm right," she snapped.

"I wish it wasn't this way."

"You're the one who makes it this way. It doesn't have to be like this. You can just drop it, like normal people do. Admit you got beat. Get over your bitterness about this case and quit blaming it for costing you all those promotions. Live the life you've got left so this doesn't tear you apart—tear *us* apart. I want to enjoy the time I have left with you."

He nodded. "I know you're right, but it's more than just about making up for my past failures—for me, this is about righting a wrong."

"News flash, Harold—this guy isn't D.B. Cooper. He's a cheap knockoff and the FBI doesn't need your help to catch him."

Harold grunted and shook his head. "I'm not so sure about that. I've been two, if not three, steps ahead of the Bureau the whole time on this case, yet they won't listen to me."

"Maybe that's your sign to move on."

"And just let this guy get away with all that he's doing? You know I can't do that."

"But you *must* move on. This case is not so important that you should risk your life. Whoever this guy is, he's dangerous. He almost got us killed last night."

"*I* almost got us killed—and he's clearly not that dangerous. I've come to the conclusion that he wants to get caught."

"Based on what?"

"He's taunting the FBI agents on the case. He wants nothing more than to become famous for what he's done, though I think he's misjudged the perception of the public as it pertains to his actions. He's universally hated instead of universally loved."

Edith sighed. "If he's taunting the FBI, let them catch him. You know my perspective of you isn't going to change whether you catch him or not."

"I know it won't—but the public's will."

"And the almighty Bureau too, huh?" She stopped and eyed him closely. "I know what you're thinking."

"If you did, Edith, you'd know to save your breath. I'm going to catch this bastard if it's the last thing I do."

She shook her head. "That's what I'm afraid of—it just may very well be the last thing you do."

# CHAPTER 29

TOMMY SPURLOCK TURNED AROUND and looked at Gordon. The engine on his plane hummed but the aircraft remained stationary.

"You ready back there, Mr. McDonald?" Spurlock asked.

Gordon didn't say a word but flashed two thumbs up and nodded.

Spurlock eased the throttle up and the plane began to rumble down the runway. Less than a minute later, they soared upward and took in a view of Seattle's sprawling metropolitan area.

Though Gordon knew this venture would create a link that might be traced back to him, he didn't care. It likely wouldn't matter. The FBI never rushed into action, making sure its cases were airtight before they made an arrest. And by the time the FBI figured it all out, he'd be long gone—just like Cooper. But he couldn't vanish just yet, not with people despising him.

Gordon glanced at his watch. On most early Sunday afternoons, he was gathered with his friends at Ridgeline, enjoying Scotch and watching the Seahawks play. But not today. Today, his friends would be watching him, though unknowingly.

Spurlock fell in behind the short line of planes gearing up to pass over CenturyLink Field. The plane in the lead toted a banner that advertised a local sports bar chain in an effort to attract fans for the Sunday- and Monday-night games. The next one carried a banner for a budget phone company. And then there was Spurlock's plane. No banner attached.

"Do you need me to climb higher?" Spurlock asked.

"No. This is good," Gordon said.

"If you jump out at this height, you might not make it."

"I'm not jumping out."

A few minutes later, Spurlock announced that they were almost over the field.

Gordon slid the door open.

"I thought you said you weren't gonna jump," Spurlock said.

"That's right. I did. And I'm not going to either."

"Well, what are you doing with the door open?"

Gordon grunted. "Just keep flying the plane. You'll see soon enough."

In a matter of seconds, Gordon hooked his harness to an O-ring built into the side of the cabin wall. He adjusted his white gloves and his beard.

"What do you think? Do I look like a good Santa Claus?" Gordon asked.

"Best I've ever seen," Spurlock said. "But please don't jump."

He turned around to see Gordon scooting closer to the edge.

"Mr. McDonald!"

"Just keep you eyes forward and fly the plane. I'm not going anywhere," Gordon said.

Gordon grabbed a giant red sack and pulled it next to him. He waved at the crowd below, close enough to tell that he'd gained their attention.

Now, time to make them love me.

Gordon reached into the bag and snagged a handful of $100 bills and tossed them out of the plane. And then another, and another.

"What the hell are you doing, man?" Spurlock shouted.

"Just fly the plane."

In the time it took Spurlock to fly his plane the length of the stadium twice, Gordon had emptied his bag. Every last $100 bill—gone.

From the roar of the crowd, they appeared to love it—just as Gordon predicted.

*Who wouldn't want to go to an NFL game and have a million dollars worth of hundred-dollar bills rain down from the sky?*

Thirty minutes later, Spurlock set his plane down on his airstrip.

"Mr. McDonald, I don't know if this was worth it," Spurlock said after he shut the engine off. "What difference does it make if I have a plane if I can't fly it again after that stunt? I'm liable to get a heavy fine from the FAA or have my pilot license suspended."

Gordon dug into bag and tossed two wads of tightly rolled cash at Spurlock. "Here's twenty grand for your troubles. Just keep your mouth shut and tell the truth."

"And what's the truth?"

"You had no idea what I was going to do and you

couldn't stop me while you were flying the plane."

Spurlock looked at the money. "That is true."

"You'll be fine. Just don't mention I came by on Friday."

***

TWO HOURS LATER, Gordon sat in the lounge at Ridgeline, nursing a glass of Scotch. He made it there in time to see the end of the game, but all the talk was about the mystery Santa Claus throwing out money from an airplane during halftime.

A man settled onto the stool next to Gordon. "Can you believe this guy? Thinks he can win over people just by throwing money at them."

Gordon took a sip and set down his glass. "It works most of the time."

"Yeah, but not when it's obvious what you're trying to do. This guy is a failed criminal who thinks he's the second coming of D.B. Cooper. He's just a hack."

Gordon shrugged. "The feds haven't caught him yet, have they? Or perhaps our criminal is a she. We have no way of knowing for sure since the feds haven't named any suspects."

The man furrowed his brow. "Where have you been, man? You haven't heard the interviews with the pilot. He claimed some man hired him and came dressed as Santa Claus."

"Good. They finally dwindled the pool of suspects in half from three hundred and twenty million."

The man chuckled. "Well, I guess that's one way to look at it." He paused and stared at his bill. "But I think they're going to catch this guy soon. He'll make a mistake somewhere. They always do."

"Not always. Don't forget D.B. Cooper is still out there."

"Well, I guess that means there's still time for him to make a mistake, too."

The man patted Gordon on the back and stood up. "Enjoy the rest of your evening."

"You, too."

Gordon focused his attention back on the television, where a local news reporter was talking with fans outside the stadium.

The first fan wore a Seahawks jersey with blue and green face paint—along with an angry scowl on his face.

The reporter, a young, fit woman with tightly cropped blonde hair, held the microphone and waited for a response from her opening question: "How did you feel about the interruption in this afternoon's game?"

*What a biased question! She should be asking how did it feel to leave the stadium with a couple hundred dollars in your pocket.*

"I don't know who this guy thinks he is," the man said. "He may have dressed up like Santa, but he was the Grinch today. Ruining the game with his stunt made me pretty angry. I wish he'd fallen out of the plane."

"Okay, sir. Thank you for your comments," said the reporter, taken aback by the vitriol. She grabbed another fan. "Ma'am, how did you feel about the forty-five minute delay this afternoon at halftime to clear the field of all that money?"

The woman shook her head. "I snagged five bills out of the air before the announcement came over the speakers that we had to give it all back or face prosecution. It was my money."

The reporter eyed the woman carefully. "But you are aware that all that money was stolen from the Federal Reserve just a few days ago?"

"Sure, but that don't mean they can just come and take my money and threaten me with jail time. I pay my taxes."

The reporter withdrew her microphone for another question. "But what do you think about the man who stole all the money?"

"He's a genius—especially for giving it away. Now there's no evidence that he ever had it. It's like the crime never existed."

*Genius. I like the sound of that.*

The reporter turned back toward the screen. "Regardless of the money, those responsible for today's stunt at halftime will also face several charges and fines, according to law enforcement officials. Dan."

Dan Walker, the smooth-talking anchor, frowned as the on-screen picture turned to him.

"Whoever this guy is jumping out of planes stealing money and then littering CenturyLink Field with it is one of the worst kinds of people," Dan stated. "I hope they catch this scumbag soon."

*Nobody asked for your opinion, Dan.*

The next segment, "What's Hot with Hannah," involved a voluptuous woman, wearing a tight blue dress and with long wavy brown hair, parading in front of the camera. Hannah held a tablet and smiled at the camera.

After several updates delivered in a countdown style about the Kardashians and Katy Perry, all of whom Gordon found obnoxious, she turned serious.

"The hottest thing on the Internet right now is

something that happened right here in our own backyard today. The top trending Twitter hashtag in the U.S. right this moment is #CoopersCreepyTwin, referencing the man who wants to be D.B. Cooper so badly but just isn't. Cooper, while also a thief, was suave and had some panache. But this guy is a poor man's Cooper who showed today how desperate he is to be loved by the public. So, join in the fun of mocking this guy on Twitter, especially those of you who had your afternoon ruined at CenturyLink Field by his antics. On a side note, I'm certain that if we didn't have that extended delay at halftime, the Seahawks would've won today instead of losing on a last-second field goal."

*Oh, now they're blaming me for the Seahawks' loss. Typical millennial crap.*

He took a long pull on his glass of Scotch and seethed. As much as he hated Hannah and her countdown, he knew she was right. He was fighting a losing battle in the court of public opinion.

*Time to cut my losses.*

# CHAPTER 30

FLYNN AND BANKS STOOD by the curb of the Seattle airport waiting for Jones to pick them up. Since they were in the air during the "Hundred Dollar Santa" incident, they didn't know anything about what happened other than the news reports.

"I'll tell you all about it when I pick you up," Jones told Banks on the phone. "I'll be there in five minutes."

The pair watched in silence as the travelers walked mindlessly into the airport, tugging luggage behind them.

"Don't you always wonder where everyone is going?" Flynn asked, gesturing toward a line of travelers.

"Those people, specifically?" she said.

"No—everyone. Where are they all going?"

She nodded. "I do think about that sometimes. Mostly I just wonder where the women with out-of-control children are going—and say a quick prayer that it isn't the same place as where I'm headed."

Flynn grinned. "I wonder if the man we're looking for is here, right now."

"If he isn't, he should be because we're going to catch him and lock him up." She stopped and pointed toward the road. "Look—there's Jones."

Jones pulled next to the curb and popped the trunk. Once Flynn and Jones stored their luggage and were buckled in, he drove toward the airport exit.

"I hope you two are ready to get back at it," Jones said. "I've got to get you caught up to speed on what happened today—and I want to hear about your trip to San Francisco."

"Before we do anything, I need to drop something off with Copperfield in forensics," Banks said.

"No problem. It's on the way."

They all exchanged their stories over the past day, swinging by the office for a brief pit stop.

"You think there's any point in talking to this pilot again?" Banks asked once she learned of Jones' plans to interview him.

Jones glanced over his shoulder and pulled onto the Interstate. "You know how local law enforcement interviews are. I feel like we need to interview him ourselves to get a feel for what this guy is about."

"What's your gut telling you?"

"That he's telling the truth, but you know the truth often contains various shades."

Flynn looked out the window and took in the conversation happening in the front seat as well as the sights of a Sunday evening in Seattle bustling along the highway. His gut told him that they were close—very close. It also told him that their suspect, whoever he was, had already made a mistake. They simply needed to catch him before he vanished like Cooper did years ago.

\*\*\*

THE DIRT ROAD leading up to Northwest Aerial Services dipped and swerved, much like Jones' driving as he fought to avoid the numerous potholes. The first stars began to twinkle beneath the dusky sky painted with fading oranges and purples. The silhouetted tail of an airplane on top of a small rise let Flynn know they were close.

"So, here's how this is going to go down," Banks said as they slowed down and pulled into the driveway. "This guy is scared. Let's make him sweat for a few minutes before we extend him any goodwill. I want to see if he'll crack without exerting too much force."

"He didn't break for the blues today," Jones said.

Banks rolled her eyes. "And your point?" She held up her badge. "This is far more frightening to most people."

Once Jones parked, they got out. Banks spotted a man tinkering on the plane about a hundred yards away.

"I bet that's our guy," she said, pointing in his direction.

They all followed her lead, trekking up the small rise to the hanger sized to fit Spurlock's Cessna 210.

"Mr. Tommy Spurlock?" she said.

"Yeah. Who's asking?" he said.

"Agent Jennifer Banks with the FBI along with Agent Chase Jones and special consultant James Flynn. We have a few questions for you, sir."

Spurlock wiped his hands on a towel and threw it aside. "I already talked with some officers earlier today."

"Well, this is linked to our case, one we're specifically investigating. Sorry for the duplication of efforts, but we need to talk."

He motioned for them to follow him back to his office. The cramped space just off the hangar floor had room for a desk, a small couch, and two chairs. Once they were all inside, Jones pulled the door shut and stood against it. Flynn settled into the couch, while Banks grabbed a chair and dragged it directly in front of his desk.

Spurlock slumped into the chair behind his desk and picked up a small metal airplane part, twirling it around in his hands and refusing to look up.

"Mr. Spurlock, what happened today over CenturyLink Field is a major FAA violation—more than one, actually," she began. "You're in danger of losing your license. Are you aware of that?"

He nodded without removing his gaze on the part in his hands.

"I need your full cooperation here. We're dealing with a dangerous criminal. And if you don't help us, we're not sure how many other people might get hurt."

Spurlock shook his head. "Well, nobody's been hurt yet, right?"

"Yet. But we want to keep it that way. When criminals like this get backed into a corner, who knows what they might do. And this guy obviously knows where you live."

Spurlock sat upright. "What do you want to know, Agent Banks?"

"I want to know how it is that you came to fly this man today," she said.

"I'll tell you what I told the cops earlier today. The man asked me to fly him over the stadium—said he wanted to take some aerial photos during the game. I had no idea he was going to open the door and start throwing out money."

She eyed him carefully. "You didn't think it was odd when he showed up in a Santa Claus outfit?"

Spurlock shrugged. "There are some weird people around here—I just thought he was in a festive mood."

"A festive mood, huh? And he lugged a giant red bag onboard and you didn't ask any questions?"

"Business has been slow lately. I can't afford to scare off any customers."

"What if he had a bomb in there?"

Spurlock shook his head. "I knew it wasn't a bomb."

"So you saw what was inside?"

"No. Not exactly. I heard it as he slung it over his shoulder. It sounded like paper and appeared really light. I didn't think he was going to throw something out. I just thought it was some publicity stunt or something to get on television."

Banks leaned forward in the chair. "So, which was it, Mr. Spurlock? A publicity stunt or a photography shoot? Seems like your story is starting to fall apart here."

He scowled. "Do I need to get a lawyer?"

"Not if you tell us the truth, though I doubt you'll be able to afford one seeing how business is so slow these days."

"Just tell us what the guy looked like?" Jones said.

"How do I really know?" Spurlock answered. "He looked like Santa Claus."

Banks folded her arms and leaned back in her chair. "And this was the first time you'd ever seen the guy?"

Spurlock nodded. "Yeah. He called me up today and asked me to do this."

"What time did he call?" she said.

"Around noon. Maybe a little after."

Flynn put his hand up in the air. "Hold up. I know a little about planes, and I'm having a hard time believing that you were able to get the plane ready for takeoff and over to the stadium that quickly if he called you that late."

"With all due respect, sir, I know a lot about planes and I've been doing this for a long time—and it doesn't take me long to get my plane prepped and ready for flight."

Flynn bobbed his head from side to side. "Yeah, maybe you've got mad skills with your airplane, but where your story falls apart for me is that this guy clearly wanted to do this during halftime. He wouldn't just start calling up places an hour before kickoff and seeing who's available."

Spurlock shrugged. "Maybe it was on a whim?"

Banks jumped back in. "And on that whim he went out and secured a Santa outfit without calling around to see if there was a company who could fly him over the stadium? Seattle's a big area, but there aren't that many pilots licensed to fly over CenturyLink Field."

Spurlock looked down again at the part in his hand, fiddling with it.

"How did he pay you?" Banks asked.

"In cash."

"Do you still have the bills with you?"

Spurlock cracked. "Okay, look. He told me not to talk to you guys. But the real story is that I fell behind on my bank payments and one of the bank representatives came out here on Friday and told me that he'd forgive my missed payments if I did him a favor."

"And you agreed to this?"

"I didn't know what he was going to do. I admit I thought it was a little strange when he showed up in a Santa Claus outfit, but I couldn't say no at that point. My wife just had surgery, and, like I said earlier, business has been slow. I was in danger of losing my plane. I didn't really have a choice."

Banks nodded. "So, what was this guy's name?"

"He said his name was William McDonald."

Banks pulled out her notepad and started jotting down notes. "Can you describe what he looked like?"

Spurlock took a deep breath. "He was balding with a goatee, Caucasian, wore glasses. And if I had to guess his age, I'd say he was in his mid-40s."

"Now, was that so difficult, Mr. Spurlock?" Banks said as she stood up.

He shook his head.

"I do appreciate your cooperation and it will be duly noted."

Spurlock's shoulders dropped as he appeared relaxed for the first time since the trio walked up to his hangar. "There is one more thing."

"What's that?" Jones asked.

"Before we got on the plane, I offered him a drink. It's sitting on that windowsill right there. He was wearing gloves so you won't get any prints other than mine, but maybe you can get something else from it."

Jones pulled out a pair of latex gloves from his pocket and held the glass. "Looks like you're driving us back to the office, Banks."

# CHAPTER 31

COLEMAN SHUFFLED INTO HIS OFFICE and made some notes after watching the evening news report about the Cooper Copycat. Because he showered the stadium with $100 bills during the Seahawks game, it actually trumped Seahawks' coverage. And Coleman couldn't remember the last time some news event trumped NFL football on the Sunday evening news when the city's beloved team had a game.

Edith stopped at the doorway and poked her head inside his office. "What are you doing, Harold?"

"Just going over a few things, honey. It's no big deal."

She chuckled. "Is that your way of telling me to leave you alone—and that you're trying to solve this case again?"

He turned around and glanced at her over his shoulder. "We've been married a long time—and you know me too well."

"I could've been married to you for only fifteen minutes and known that."

She sighed. "Just don't do anything stupid, okay?"

He nodded and waited until she left before he picked up the phone. He dialed Jones' number.

"This is Jones," came the voice on the other end.

"Agent Jones, thank goodness it's you," Coleman said.

"I was hoping we could speak again."

"Mr. Coleman, would you please leave us alone and let us do our jobs?"

"I would—if you were doing them well. It seems like you keep dropping the ball at every turn, and you're not listening to me."

"Why do we need to listen to you? You say the same thing every time, over and over?"

Banks walked over to Jones' desk. "Who is it?" she mouthed.

Jones put his hand on the receiver. "Crazy old man Coleman."

She snapped her fingers. "Here, let me talk to him."

Jones sighed. "Whatever. He's your problem now."

Banks took the phone and settled down into Jones' chair. "Mr. Coleman, do you realize how difficult it is to do our jobs when you keep bothering us?"

"I can empathize with you—I really can. But I know who's behind all this."

"And who's that?"

"If I've told you once, I've told you a hundred times—it's Carlton Gordon."

Banks exhaled a long breath. "Look, Mr. Coleman, I checked out his alibi after you told us that last time and he passed with flying colors."

"Well, he tried to kill me Friday night."

"Really? That doesn't seem to be how he operates."

"What I mean is that he tried to run me off the road—and succeeded. Fortunately, it only resulted in a bashed up fender and a nasty bruise for Edith when the airbag deployed."

"And you were sharing the road with him because—?"

"Well, maybe I was tailing him."

She sighed. "Did you report this to the police?"

"There was no need. The car was still drivable, not to mention it happened on a dirt road."

"And which dirt road was that?"

"One leading right up to Northwest Aerial Services."

She paused. "Interesting—but you know I can't use a single shred of what you just told me in court. And even if we could, it's all circumstantial."

"But at some point, Agent Banks, you know that where there's smoke, there's fire."

"I'm in the business of putting away criminals, not speculating—and in order to do my job, I need more than coincidences and hunches."

Coleman grunted. "If you don't do something about this guy, he's going to end up hurting someone."

"Thank you for the call, Mr. Coleman. I'll look into this."

"Good luck."

Banks hung up and let out a string of expletives. "I swear that man is gonna get himself killed if he keeps this up.

She marched down the hall to forensics. "Jones, grab your coat. We need to pay Carlton Gordon a visit again."

Jones let out an exasperated breath. "Look, just take your special consultant. I really don't have time right now."

"What's so important that you can't break away?"

"I'm working back here with Copperfield, trying to see if we can pull some prints off this glass the pilot gave us."

She chuckled. "Trying to break into forensics now?"

"If being an agent doesn't work out, I want to have another career option in the Bureau so I don't end up like Coleman."

"We'll be back soon."

\*\*\*

FLYNN LATCHED HIS SEATBELT and settled into the passenger's seat of Banks' car. As the engine roared to life with the twist of her key, Banks looked at Flynn. He had his nose buried near his armpit, inhaling large breaths through his nose.

"What are you doing?" she asked.

He didn't answer, switching the target of his sniffing to the front of his shirt. He pinched it with his index finger and thumb and raised it close to his nose.

"You might be smelling the stench from the dead guy whose scent I still catch from time to time. He was only in the truck for three days, but I never thought it could get so bad so fast."

"You often travel with dead companions?"

"Just one of the job hazards, I'm afraid."

He cut his eyes toward her. "Is that the reason you have at least a half dozen scented Christmas trees in this vehicle?"

"I try. I really do. But the odor of a dead man is difficult to mask."

"I put on some cologne this morning to see how long it would last throughout the day."

"Depends on what kind you put on."

"What about Stallion?"

She laughed. "I'm not a cologne expert, but I know what it smells like—and it's obvious that you aren't wearing it. I'm thinking maybe some designer cologne sold in bulk at Macy's."

"I didn't buy it in bulk. And I didn't get it at Macy's. One more strike and you're out."

"Maybe a brand you could pick up from Wal-Mart then?"

"Look, this stuff wasn't cheap." He paused. "But it did come in a rather large bottle."

"So it was in bulk?"

He shrugged. "Perhaps. Define bulk."

"If you have enough to take a bath in it—it's bulk."

Flynn looked up and thought for a moment. "Okay, maybe it *is* bulk. But it'd be a tiny bathtub."

"Don't worry—if Gordon is wearing Stallion cologne, I'll know it."

"I'm more concerned about him wearing a side piece than cologne."

"Fair point. Good thing I've got a gun—and I'm a pretty good shot." She smiled at him and winked.

Flynn looked out the window and sighed. The conversation, while a necessary one, was a speed bump to him. He wanted to fast forward to the end—the part where the criminal is revealed.

"Am I boring you, Flynn?" she asked.

He shook his head and bit his lip.

"I know. You're probably staring out that window right now and pining away for a television interview."

He glanced at her. "Hardly."

"What? Don't you love having millions of followers

who hang on your every word?"

Flynn shrugged. "Sure. That's kinda cool. But that's just a byproduct of what I do."

"And what exactly *do* you do?"

"I expose conspiracies."

She bobbed her head back and forth. "Well, as far as conspiracies go, this one is pretty cut and dry."

"You never know. Some people still think D.B. Cooper was an inside job."

She flipped her blinker on as they stopped at a traffic light. "Some people think aliens are running everything here."

Flynn couldn't help but chuckle. "I know. Those people make up eighty percent of my fans." He sighed and sat back in his seat. "There's just something about this case that's just not right."

"Think we're about to get our answer?"

"We'll find out—and it'll be the end of Coleman torturing us."

A grin spread across her face. "Ain't that the truth?"

Several minutes later, Banks pulled into a vacant spot along the street, across from the entrance to Carlton Gordon's condo. They both got out of her vehicle and crossed the road.

"Ready for this?" Banks asked. "One way or another, we're going to get some answers."

Banks rapped hard on Gordon's door.

"Who is it?" Gordon asked.

"It's Agent Banks."

Gordon's displeasure, marked by a slight groan and accompanied by a heavy sigh, could be heard through the door.

"Just a moment."

"This ought to be pleasant," Flynn said.

The door opened and Gordon appeared, his hands on his hips. "What is this about, detective?"

"Agent. It's Agent Banks."

"Whatever," he said, waving them inside. "I don't care what they call you as long as you end this endless harassment once and for all." He turned toward them after he shut the door. "Please, have a seat."

They all sat down on the couches in his living room, Flynn and Banks on the smaller love seat and Gordon on the long couch all alone.

"I'm sorry about this, Mr. Gordon," she said. "I hope you understand. We just need to eliminate you once again."

"This is getting old, *Agent* Banks."

"I understand." She pulled out her notebook. "So, where were you this afternoon?"

He rolled his eyes. "I was at the 12th Street Bistro and Pub watching football with some friends."

"Any chance you've got names and contact information for those friends?"

He nodded. "Let me write them down for you." He disappeared from the room.

While he was gone, Flynn took the opportunity to walk around and check out Gordon's digs. Banks remained on the couch, scratching out a few notes on her pad.

Flynn glanced at the mail on the counter. It appeared to be nothing more than a handful of bills. Yet it was the painting on the far wall that captured his attention—"The Incredible Journey of the Caird" by Austin Dwyer.

Gordon walked back into the room.

Flynn turned around. "Original?"

Gordon nodded. "I love maritime paintings. The rough waters and the struggle for survival—there's just something about those images. I could sit and stare at them all day."

"Life's never easy, even when it's supposed to be." He paused. "You sail?"

Gordon shook his head. "I try to stay away for any activity that might result in my death."

"Like jumping out of airplanes?"

Gordon shot Flynn a look. "I definitely stay away from that activity."

"Good," Banks said, taking from Gordon the piece of paper with the names of his football buddies. "Stay away from anything that takes you out of town, too."

"Why?" Gordon said. "Am I under suspicion for a crime?"

Banks rubbed her forehead with her left hand. "Give me a few more minutes and I'll tell you."

"Fair enough," Gordon answered. "I'm confident you'll be calling me back with news that I'm cleared so I can get out of here for a while."

"Big plans elsewhere?" Flynn asked.

"I take a ski trip to Switzerland about this time every year."

Banks held up the paper and locked eyes with Gordon. "Thanks for your cooperation." She turned and looked at Flynn. "Let's go."

"What's your favorite maritime painting, Mr. Gordon," Flynn asked, ignoring Banks' directive.

A wide grin spread across Gordon's face. "That's

easy—Hendrick Cornelisz Vroom's *Dutch Ships Ramming Spanish Galleys off the Flemish Coast.*"

"So, which one are you—the Dutch or the Spanish?"

Gordon's eyes narrowed. "I'm always the victor."

"Interesting. I always thought the victor kept his spoils," Flynn said before spinning around and joining Banks at the door.

"I hope you catch him," Gordon said.

"Me, too," Banks said before pulling the door shut.

She didn't say a word until they were in the elevator.

"What was that all about?" Banks said. "You're here to help me with this investigation, not jeopardize it."

"He knows exactly what he's doing—and you know it, too."

She held up her hand. "Let's check out these names he gave us before we draw any conclusions."

A few minutes later in her car, Banks was furiously dialing the list of contacts Gordon presented her with. Caller after caller described a similar afternoon, one in which they hung out at the same bar and watched football. They weren't all exactly the same, but there were no statements that drew her suspicion.

After the fourth call, she sighed. With shoulders slumped, she declared, "Looks like Gordon wasn't in that plane this afternoon."

"Jones must be right about Coleman, then. He's certainly crazy."

"Perhaps."

"Okay, so if it wasn't Gordon, who was up there in that plane this afternoon? Because it had to be somebody he knew if he's behind all this."

Banks shrugged. "I've got no idea." She paused as she cranked the ignition on her car. "But I did learn something interesting about Gordon on our little visit this evening."

"What's that?"

"He wears Stallion cologne."

# CHAPTER 32

ON MONDAY MORNING, Gordon awoke with a sharp pain in his gut. More coughing and spitting up blood—and it was getting worse. He threw on his bathrobe and shuffled toward the kitchen. A glass of water increased the pain, forcing him to call his doctor again.

"Hi, this is Carlton Gordon, one of Doctor Watts' patients. I was wondering if I might be able to get an appointment with him this morning," he said to the cheery receptionist.

"Can you tell me what kind of symptoms you're experiencing?" she asked.

Gordon briefly described them and awaited an answer.

"Hold please."

Gordon drummed his fingers on the kitchen counter. He knew the end was rapidly approaching—he just had no idea it'd be *this* rapid or *this* painful. Besides, he still had work to do.

After a couple of minutes, the line clicked.

"Mr. Gordon?" asked the smooth voice on the other end.

"Yes, Doctor Watts. Thank you for taking my call. I didn't think I'd actually get to speak with you on the phone—just hoping to squeeze in a visit."

"It's very busy today here in the office. What can I do for you?"

Gordon took a deep breath. "The pain in my stomach is getting worse. I woke up this morning and coughed up a bunch of blood."

"More so than usual?"

"Yes, much more. It feels like I'm walking around with a knife jabbing me in the midsection."

Dr. Watts sighed. "I'm afraid there's not much more I can do for you, Mr. Gordon, other than prescribe a more powerful pain killer." He paused. "Have you spoken with your next of kin about your condition?"

"It's not exactly something I've been itching to do."

"Don't put it off until it's too late."

"It's that bad, huh?"

"If you're accurately describing your symptoms, yes."

"I was hoping you wouldn't say that."

"I'm sorry, Mr. Gordon. I wish there was more I could do for you at this point. Had we caught it earlier—" He let his words hang in the air.

"I understand. Thank you for your time."

"You're welcome. Stay on the line and give our receptionist all your pharmacy information and I'll get that prescription put in for you."

Gordon thanked his doctor and answered all the questions the receptionist had before hanging up.

He hated Mondays as they were—and starting one off with this kind of news escalated his hatred.

\*\*\*

WHEN GORDON ENTERED the break room around ten o'clock, he was hoping that he was wrong about his premonitions regarding his stunt the day before.

*The newscasters are just making a bigger deal out of this than it is. They're looking to blame someone and make us all feel better about the Seahawks' crumby play yesterday.*

But that wasn't the case at all. His own employees ditched the Cooper Copycat moniker altogether.

"They're calling him the Robin Hood Santa," one of the men in the break room said.

"Yeah, well he's a poor imitation of both," another woman responded. "Robin Hood at least stole from greedy bastards—and Santa had the decency to slip into your house and leave something, not litter it all over the top of your house."

Everyone in the room chuckled. Had it not been so disturbing, an uproarious laughter might have come from the room. Gordon forced himself to laugh with them.

"When they catch this guy, I can't wait to see what they're going to do to him," another man quipped just as Gordon stood up.

"And what are you hoping for, Trent?" Gordon asked the man. "A confession? A televised execution *Hunger Games* style? A public flogging? A good old-fashioned tarring and feathering? Hot oil?"

The man, taken aback by Gordon's harsh tone, stared at his boss with mouth agape.

"Well, which is it?" Gordon asked again.

"Geez, lighten up. We're all just having a little fun here. Nobody is out for blood."

Gordon headed toward the exit. "Could've fooled me.

I'm thinking you're the one who needs to lighten up. It's just money. Nobody's gotten hurt."

Back in his office, Gordon seethed again. No amount of goodwill would help him curry favor with a bloodthirsty public. He couldn't believe he'd been so wrong about how people would react to his stunt—and not only his initial one, but his stunt to smooth things over.

Yet as he leaned back in his chair and pondered his next move, the good news was that they couldn't trace the money back to him—not now anyway. There was hardly any of it left and he'd made sure they wouldn't find it.

He decided what he would do—and he needed to go home and prepare.

Exiting his office, he walked past his secretary's desk before doubling over in pain.

"Mr. Gordon, are you okay? Do you need me to call an ambulance?" she asked as she knelt next to him.

He motioned for her to hand him the trash can.

Moments later he spit up more blood and staggered to his feet. "I'll be all right. I just need to go home and rest a bit. Please cancel all my meetings for the rest of the afternoon."

His sickness provided an opportunity to sneak home without appearing suspicious. The last thing he needed was to spend another minute explaining why he felt so awful.

For his plan to work, it required immediacy—and there wasn't much more time.

# CHAPTER 33

BY 5 A.M., FLYNN HAD APPEARED on several morning news programs, including CNN's *New Day* and ABC's *Good Morning America*. The cable news cycle couldn't get enough of this story—and neither could network news. What should have been a lazy Monday morning dominated by fluffy holiday segments, was instead overrun by talking heads dissecting the brazen criminal activity of an elusive thief. Flynn treaded carefully, answering what he could with information that was somewhat public while keeping the juiciest portions to himself. At the end of the day, he still had a story to write, and the more exclusive the better for his editor and *The National*.

The perky blonde on ABC narrowed her eyes and leaned forward for her final question. "So, Mr. Flynn, is this guy going to be the second coming of D.B. Cooper or is the FBI going to catch him?"

Flynn shrugged. "I'm a reporter, not a prophet. But what I can tell you is the FBI isn't going to leave a stone unturned. If he makes a mistake, it'll be the last one he makes as a free man. That much you can bet on."

"Chilling words," she said with a wink before introducing another hard news feature about the security at the U.S. Federal Reserve printing locations.

Flynn left the ABC affiliate studio at KOMO and proceeded to the FBI field office a few miles away. Banks awaited him with a cup of coffee.

"What's this?" Flynn asked as he looked at the cup she offered him.

"A small token of gratitude for your help on this case," she said, releasing the cup into his hand. "You've been more helpful than you know—and I saw you on television this morning. I figured you might need a jolt to get you going."

He smiled. "How thoughtful." A short pause. "I guess you haven't read what I wrote this morning."

Her eyes widened and she drew back. "No, I must've missed it."

Flynn refused to take his joke any further. "Don't worry. I haven't written a word. I'm hoping to write a wrap-up today recounting everything that's happened in this case so readers can see that this isn't the same as D.B. Cooper—and that this is no government conspiracy or inside job."

"I hope you get to write that today as well, but something tells me we've still got a long way to go."

Flynn checked his watch. It wasn't quite nine o'clock.

"Where's Jones?" he asked.

"He's testifying in court this morning," she said.

"Which case?"

"Some witness protection case."

"And who's that?"

She eyed Flynn closely. "Are you testing me? You know I can't talk about that—and I wouldn't, even if I could."

"Fair enough. Got any other news?"

Before she could answer, her desk phone buzzed.

"This is Banks."

"Agent Banks, this is Copperfield. We need you to come down here to forensics as soon as possible. There's something you need to see."

She hung up and turned to Flynn. "Come with me. Forensics has something."

\*\*\*

IN THE FORENSICS LAB, Copperfield greeted Banks at the door with a printout on top of a manila folder.

"What am I looking at here?" she asked.

"Something far more than a coincidence."

Her eyebrows shot up. "Oh?"

"Yeah," he said, pointing at two boxes next to each other. "I analyzed the cigarettes you gave me yesterday with the ones we collected from the original plane."

"And?"

"And the DNA left behind proves to be a perfect match."

She nodded. "Anything in the database?"

He took the folder from her and opened it up. "Apparently, it's from this guy."

Banks stared at the picture of an African-American man. She held it up so Flynn could see it. "Look familiar?"

"Doc?"

She bobbed her head up and down. "The one and only."

"So, the man with Stallion cologne is our guy."

She stuffed all the papers inside the folder and slapped it against her leg. "We need to talk to Thurston."

Flynn's imagination ran wild as he tried to imagine how

Gordon could've committed such a crime and coerced so many people into lying for him. The truth is that couldn't be the case. With as many people as they talked to, someone was bound to snitch. The amount of vitriol hurled at the Cooper Copycat by the general public made it difficult to believe at least one person wouldn't renege on their earlier confession of seeing him. Chances are *somebody* would do it. Something about it all now felt so rehearsed and perfect.

"He's been playing us this whole time," Flynn said.

Banks squinted as she looked at Flynn. "But how? It just doesn't make sense. How could he have pulled this all off? Even if he did it, I'm not sure this case would ever hold up in court. And Thurston won't let us prosecute unless we've got a rock solid case against him."

"He's bound to slip up sooner or later."

She held up her index finger. "If he keeps going—and I'm not so sure he's done. We've practically recouped all the money already."

"But the FBI isn't as concerned with the money as they are with their image. Catching the criminal on such a high profile case like this will put Thurston in line for a promotion. If he thinks this guy is the one, he'll risk it to prove it one way or another."

"Perhaps, but he's a dedicated rule follower. He's not going to jeopardize his current standing with the Bureau just to earn a cushier job."

The elevator dinged, alerting them that they had arrived at the proper floor.

"I guess we're about to find out."

Flynn followed Banks down the hall until they arrived at Thurston's office.

"Come in," Thurston said, acknowledging Banks' firm knock.

They both entered his office and sat down across from him.

"I hope you've got some good news, Banks," he said. "So far, Monday has been a crap fest."

She tossed the folder onto his desk. "Read this."

Thurston opened the folder. "What am I looking at here?"

"Forensics' analysis of the cigarettes found on the plane on Monday and the cigarettes we collected from a man named Doc on a street corner in San Francisco, near the apartment of the woman whose access card was used to by-pass security."

"And?"

"They're a match."

Thurston slammed the folder shut. "Geez, Banks. Can't you get me anything useful? Did you tell me yesterday this old guy was blind?"

She nodded. "True. But he also told me whoever handed him the cigarettes wore Stallion cologne."

"Hell, everybody wears that crap these days."

"Perhaps, but that's what Carlton Gordon was wearing when I interviewed him last night and checked out his alibi. An interesting coincidence, don't you think?"

"Not enough to get a conviction, which is all I care about." He paused. "Besides, didn't his alibi check out?"

"It did, but there's something going on here. I can feel it. It's more than just a coincidence."

He stood up and pointed at the door. "Well, go bring him in here and make him sweat so we can get something to put his ass in jail, if he's the one who's behind all this."

She and Flynn stood up and exited.

"And Banks," Thurston said. "Don't come back empty handed. We need something actionable—even if it's not him. We've gotta catch this guy like yesterday."

She nodded. "Do I need to grab another agent since Jones is in court this morning?"

He shook his head. "You and Flynn seem to make a formidable pair." He flashed a brief smile. "And Flynn, if you ever get tired of waking up before six in the morning and talking to airhead reporters, I think I might be able to find a place for you here."

"That's a generous offer, sir. I'll keep that in mind if things go south in journalism."

He waved at them. "Good luck."

As they walked toward her desk, Banks looked at Flynn. "What's your gut telling you?"

"There's something else at work here, that's for sure. Whenever something looks this obvious—but is so obvious it isn't—I jump to another conclusion."

"Which is what?"

"That Gordon has help. I feel like he's behind it, but someone has to be helping him. How else could he do all of this?"

"Think it's somebody at the club?"

Flynn shrugged. "Could be. It'd make sense since that's where he supposedly was during the time of the first crime."

She stuffed the folder into her bag. "But what about the second crime?"

"Not sure about that—but perhaps his accomplice was the one who committed it."

"And the cigarettes?"

"I haven't figured that one out yet, but I suppose there's an answer."

As Banks grabbed her keys, her phone rang. "Banks."

After a few moments, she held the phone away from her. "Speak of the devil," she whispered to Flynn. "It's Edwin Goodyear from the Ridgeline Golf and Polo Club."

She turned on the speaker and put the phone in the cradle. "Mr. Goodyear," she began, "I wanted to let you know you're on speaker now with me and Mr. James Flynn, who's consulting on this case."

"Okay," he muttered. "Anyway, I was following up from my phone call from a couple of days ago."

"I apologize, Mr. Goodyear, but you'll have to refresh my memory since you didn't speak with me. Who did you talk to?"

"An Agent Jones, I think?"

"He's not here today, so I'm afraid you'll have to catch me up to speed on the conversation."

Goodyear sighed. "I told your agent that Carlton Gordon is the guy. I know it."

"And how do you know this?"

"I had hired a private investigator to follow Gordon around due to suspicions I had about him in some other areas—and he took pictures of him at an airfield on days he was supposedly playing polo at the club. Your agent said he was going to look into this."

"Well, perhaps he is, but we've had a lot going on here lately and Agent Jones is in court today, testifying in another case. I'll speak with him about this once I see him later today."

She hung up and studied her desk. "Why wouldn't Jones leave me a note about that?"

Flynn scanned her desk. "It seems like he did," he said, reaching beneath a manual on her desk and dislodging a phone conversation note. "I believe it's right here."

She took the note from Flynn and read it. "Okay, so I must've missed it." She flashed a hint of a smile. "Now all we've got to do is press him until he gives up his accomplice. This will make Thurston a happy man."

"And me, too," Flynn said. "I'll finally be able to put this story to bed and get onto more sensational conspiracies."

"What?" Banks asked with an incredulous look on her face. "This isn't sensational enough for you? The Cooper Copycat or Robin Hood Santa?"

"Nothing beats what I'm looking into next."

Her eyes lit up. "Oh, do tell."

Flynn wagged his finger at her. "Not so fast. This one is top secret."

"Even for an FBI agent?"

He nodded. "You'll have to wait like the rest of the world."

"Well, aren't you a spoil sport?"

"Let's go get your man—or should I say, men?" Flynn shot back.

\*\*\*

THEIR TRIP TO BANK OF OLYMPIA was a short one after learning that Gordon went home early due to an illness.

"Think he's up to something or really at home?" Banks asked as she drove toward Gordon's condo.

"You can't fake spitting up blood," Flynn said. Then he paused. "Well, you can because I've done it, but that's some serious commitment to the craft. Not sure that he's there yet."

"I never underestimate these people," she said. "They surprise me all the time."

A few minutes later, they parked in a private garage a block from Gordon's condo. The stiff breeze nipped at them as they hustled down the street.

"Smells like it's about to snow," Flynn said.

"Snow has a distinct smell?"

"Yeah, I know. Everything smells like rain to you people here in Seattle since that's all you ever get. But I can tell it's about to snow."

"It's still a little early in the season for snow."

"It's after Thanksgiving. All bets are off."

She shook her head and laughed before skipping up the steps and entering Gordon's condo building. After a deep breath, she knocked on the door.

Several moments of silence preceded heavy and methodical steps across the hardwood floor of Gordon's apartment. She forced a smile as she glanced at Flynn, whose eyes went back and forth as he waited for the door to open.

The peephole darkened.

"Ah, Detective Banks and Mr. Flynn, how nice of you to drop by," he said as the door swung open.

"It's Agent Banks," she said as she stepped inside.

"And what brings you here today?" he said, slipping past them to shut the door.

"We have a few questions for you," she said.

"Oh? What kind?"

"For starters, we have physical proof that you were at a regional airstrip when you claimed to be playing polo at the Ridgeline Golf and Polo Club on the days the Cooper Copycat struck."

He gestured for them to sit down as he took a seat directly across from them on a smaller sofa. "Cooper Copycat? Mr. Flynn, certainly doesn't call the suspect that."

"You read my stuff?" Flynn asked as he settled onto the couch next to Banks. "I'm honored."

Gordon straightened several magazines on the coffee table. "It's not a compliment," he said, his tone turning harsh.

"Hey, now. No need to get combative," Flynn said.

"Who's getting combative?" Gordon said, before he stood up and lunged toward them.

Before Flynn or Banks could move, Gordon pulled a small canister from his pocket and sprayed a liquid in their faces. The pair collapsed to the floor.

# CHAPTER 34

GORDON LUGGED THE BODIES of Flynn and Banks into Tommy Spurlock's plane and climbed inside. He signaled for Spurlock to go.

"Why are you doing this?" Spurlock asked as he eased down the bumpy grass airstrip.

Gordon laughed. "You wouldn't understand. It's complicated." He paused. "It's the same line you'll use when FBI agents come to your house and ask why you chose to go along with my plan."

"No, it's not that complicated—I'm being blackmailed into doing it."

"You think you don't have a choice, Tommy? Everybody has a choice. Go ahead turn the plane around. You can do it if you want to. But you made your choice a few months ago when you decided to stiff the bank—and now you're going to *pay*."

Spurlock spun the plane around at the end of the airstrip and opened up the throttle. The plane bounced and bobbed until it lurched upward and soared over the vast green vegetation.

"Please don't push them out of the plane," Spurlock begged. "I don't want to be an accomplice to murder."

"Where would the fun be in that? I'd never do any such

thing." He reached up and put his hand on Spurlock's shoulder. "And just remember, Tommy? If you get back here and tell the FBI where I am, our little deal is off. And don't think I won't know."

Gordon withdrew his hand and glanced toward the western horizon. It wasn't quite four-thirty in the afternoon, but the sun was slipping fast.

*Perfect.*

He tugged on his straps to make sure they were taut, wincing as he did. Despite the fact that the endorphins coursing through his body had given him a natural high he never expected, it couldn't offset the pain in his gut. He spit up some more blood before taking a deep breath.

*Time to get to work.*

He slapped Flynn and Banks in the face a few times each.

"It's time to wake up!"

Flynn awoke first, squinting at Gordon as he tried to gain his bearings. Banks followed suit a few moments later but appeared to reach a level of awareness much more quickly. Her eyes widened as she glanced out the open door on the plane.

"Welcome back to consciousness, Agent Banks," Gordon said.

Flynn realized his situation and lunged at Gordon, only to discover he was handcuffed to an O-ring jutting out from the plane's cabin wall.

"Are you crazy?" Flynn asked. "What are you doing?"

Gordon chuckled and said, "Maybe you should be asking yourself that question. I'm not the one about to get thrown out of an airplane without a parachute on."

Flynn glanced down at his chest. No harness was connected to him, though Banks had one on.

"What? You didn't think I was going to make this too easy on you, now did you?" Gordon said as he chortled at his own comment.

Banks finally got over her initial shock. "You're insane."

"Perhaps, but you have to admit this is far more interesting than any other case you've had since you've been at the Bureau. Right now, you're probably wondering to yourself: *How did Carlton Gordon pull this off? His alibis check out. There was nothing in his past to make us think he would turn into a psychopath.* And you're right to wonder such things. It makes no sense on the surface. But the truth always lies beneath."

"Spare us the psychological babble. You just lie," Banks said, seething.

"I've answered your questions with candor—"

"And lies."

"Well, perhaps I may have exaggerated certain truths from time to time, but it was all in good fun to keep you on your toes—which you obviously aren't now or perhaps never really were. Those cuffs anchoring you to one another and to the plane suggest that you've been asleep this whole time—just like Harold Coleman was years ago when he was supposed to be tracking down D.B. Cooper."

"Is that what this is all about?" Flynn asked. "You paying homage to some ridiculous cult hero by trying to be like him?"

"I found D.B. Cooper's successful evasion from the FBI to be something of interest, but I'm certainly not celebrating it."

"You're certainly not copying it either," Flynn hissed. "What kind of pansy steals away in the cargo hold and considers himself as an equal to D.B. Cooper? Worse than that, the public hates you. You're despised and mocked by all. They'll write songs about you, all right, just like they did with Cooper. But the ones they write about you will be denigrating for generations to come."

"On the contrary, Mr. Flynn, I did something Cooper never did: I stole money twice and jumped from airplanes— and never got caught."

"Not yet anyway," Banks said.

"Even if you catch me, I'll be like Cooper in the fact that you'll never get to take me to trial. Convicting me after I die would be a hollow pursuit."

"Suicide by law enforcement," Flynn said. "Another original pursuit."

"Watch your tone, especially about things of which you don't know." He clapped his hands. "Now, I suppose you are both wondering what you're doing up here and how you're going to get down, so I'll keep it simple by answering these questions in reverse order. First, you get down by jumping out of this airplane. Second, you're both up here to disprove a long proffered theory by the FBI that D.B. Cooper died when he jumped into the dark just west of the Gifford Pinchot National Forest."

"What?" Banks asked. "I'm not some expert paratrooper like some people suspect Cooper was."

Gordon held up his index finger. "True, but your partner in crime here is, sort of."

"But I don't have a parachute on, wise guy," Flynn snapped.

Gordon shrugged. "I know. Where would the fun be in that?"

"I'm giving you a fifteen-minute head start. Good luck."

Gordon worked quickly to detach Flynn and Banks from one another and release Banks from the wall.

"Bon voyage!" he said as he shoved her out of the plane.

"What are you doing?" Flynn asked. "She's got no experience."

"Trust me," Gordon said with a wink. "This ain't her first rodeo." He released Flynn from his cuffs and pulled out a handgun, training it on his captive. He motioned with his gun toward the open door. "But you better get out there quick before she pulls the chord and you meet an untimely demise. Not that I care—I've never had much use for journalists, especially one who's a snitch."

Flynn didn't move.

"Better move," Gordon said, firing a shot through the opening. "In another minute or two, you won't be able to see her."

Flynn shuffled sideways with his back to the cabin wall. When he reached the opening, he swallowed hard and did a backflip out of the plane.

"Fly in a circle," Gordon said to Spurlock. "I want to be over this exact same spot in fifteen minutes so I can jump." He paused. "Nah. Make it ten. Gotta keep this interesting."

# CHAPTER 35

FLYNN COULD SEE BANKS flying through the air toward the ground in front of him. Though she'd admitted to parachuting once out of an airplane, he hoped she'd keep her cool and not pull the ripcord too early. He watched her sinking toward the ground, arms and legs flailing.

Flynn tucked in his arms and held his legs tightly together. He was gaining on her, and he could only hope it would be in time.

The ground rushed toward him as he tried to stay focused. *Grab onto Banks, pull the cord—and pray.*

It sounded simple enough, but doing it at a speed of two hundred miles per hour increased the level of difficulty, especially when Banks was only traveling around one hundred and twenty miles per hour.

*Steady. Steady.*

Flynn could see her about fifty feet below him. He started to slow his descent by spreading open his arms and legs.

*Whoosh!*

Banks pulled the chute and her body lurched upwards toward Flynn.

He opened his arms and reached for her, nearly sending her spinning. His immediate need was to grab onto Banks, but his next priority was stabilizing the parachute.

Banks screamed as he hit her, nearly knocking her horizontal. Flynn latched on just below her waist. He then slipped slowly down her legs about a foot to help stabilize her. The downward motion of his weight prevented her from entering into a spiral and killing them both.

After it was evident that disaster had been avoided, Flynn wormed his way up Banks' body until he could look her in the face.

"Does this count as a second date?" she asked. "Because if it does, I really want to see other people."

Flynn chuckled as they drifted down through the chilled late autumn air. As they descended, he noticed snowflakes falling with them. "Don't you find this somewhat romantic? You, me, snowflakes and—"

"What's that smell?" she asked.

A sudden jarring motion stunned Flynn before he could answer and he lost his grip.

His cries echoed throughout the woods and ended with a thud.

"Flynn! Are you okay?"

"Never better," Flynn said, dusting off the dirt from his pants. "Just a short drop. You're almost here."

Flynn spoke too soon.

A gnarly pine branch snagged Banks' chute, leaving her suspended in the air.

"You got a knife?" she asked.

Flynn could barely see her silhouette hanging from the tree. "If I had a knife, neither of us would be standing here right now. Just work your way out of the harness. I'll catch you."

He estimated that she was about fifteen feet off the ground. If he could catch her and break her fall, she'd be fine.

After a few minutes, she managed to loosen her harness and climb out by pulling up on the parachute straps. Once she shook her legs free of the harness, she looked at Flynn.

"You ready for me?"

"Make the leap."

She let go and fell. Flynn caught her initially but fell backward over a stump and tumbled to the ground.

"Wuss," she said. "I thought you were stronger than that."

"A thank you would be nice."

"From you, yes. It was my chute after all that saved you." She stopped. "Again, what's that smell?"

Flynn wrinkled his nose. "I'm not sure, but it's rancid."

"You think Gordon was kidding about giving us a fifteen-minute head start?"

"I'm not interested in sticking around to find out."

"Agreed. And I'll do anything to get away from that stench."

"That smells like raw meat or something."

They walked for a few yards, unable to escape the odor.

"Where is that coming from?" Banks asked. "I think it's you."

Flynn laughed. "Yes. It's always the guy. Guys just stink, so it must be me, naturally."

She walked up to him and sniffed his shirt. "It *is* you."

He eyed her closely. "I don't know. You got some funk going on yourself." He walked up and sniffed her shirt. "Nah. I think it's you."

She grabbed her shirt by the corner over her shoulder and inhaled a whiff. "Uhh. It's on both of us. That is disgusting."

"Let's just keep moving."

She stopped. "Do we even know where we are?"

"If I had to guess, I'd say we're somewhere near Ariel, Washington."

"And why's that?"

"Because that's where D.B. Cooper supposedly landed that night when he jumped out of the plane."

Banks' eyebrows shot upward. "And you think he's trying to recreate the experience?"

"I think that's what he's been doing all along—and we were just a bonus."

"So where to next?"

"If memory serves me correctly, I think if we travel along the water in a westward direction, we'll eventually reach some civilization and get out of here."

"Sounds like a plan," she said.

They tramped off into the woods, searching for the water. Snowflakes continued to fall as they moved west.

After twenty minutes of walking in silence, Banks stopped.

"Did you hear that?" she asked.

"Hear what?" Flynn said.

A short low growl broke the peaceful evening.

"*That*," she said.

"Yep. I heard it that time."

"What do you think it is?" she asked.

"I don't have to ask. I know *exactly* what that sound is—and you're not gonna like it."

# CHAPTER 36

COLEMAN DIALED BANKS' DIRECT LINE and waited as the phone rang—six times and then to voicemail. "You've reached the office of Agent Jennifer Banks. I can't take your call right now, but if you'll leave a voicemail with your name and number, I'll be happy to call you back at my earliest convenience. Or you can send me an email at jbanks at FBI dot gov."

"Agent Banks, this is Harold Coleman," he began. "I've called you and left you several messages. Please call me back. I want to find out what you learned last night. I've got a bad feeling about you right now and I want to make sure you're okay. Please call me back."

He hung up but was startled almost immediately by Edith.

"Harold, who are you talking to in there," she yelled from the other room.

"Oh, no one," he said. "Just leaving a voicemail."

"For who? That FBI agent again? Will you please just give it a rest?"

He loved Edith, but he resented the fact that—like most women—she had bat ears and could detect the slightest rise in anxiety from his breathing patterns. And if he was actually making intelligible noises? Forget about it. She'd be able to psychoanalyze his behavior from that alone.

"No, just leaving a message for the body shop, asking about when we can bring the car in to get it repaired." He lied. He felt guilty about it for a second. But when she finally stopped nagging him for a moment about his continued contact with Agent Banks, he took a deep breath and smiled. Peace. That's all he wanted. The same feeling he had on the outside right now, he wanted on the inside, too.

He hobbled down the stairs into the cellar to review his crime map. Despite retiring years ago from the FBI, he couldn't break the habit of creating a visual map of any crime in which he was interested. Most of the time, it would be about a crime in some other part of the country and he'd never have any contact with the case. Edith hounded him about it until he agreed to stop making the maps in their bedroom and make them downstairs in the basement. It was a pain to climb the stairs, but not nearly as annoying as taking continued flack for it.

Methodically, his eyes moved across the board he'd created. It was part historical record and part psychological profile. In order to know the *why* of the crime, he needed to know the *who*. And the *who* baffled him.

Then a thought hit him and he started to piece it all together. This was a crime committed by a fan, a disgruntled fan—perhaps even a fan trying to one-up the original criminal. Carlton Gordon admired D.B. Cooper and his genius to pull off such a crime, but he also begrudged him for remaining hidden all these years.

"What's he afraid of?" Coleman asked. "Getting caught, of course."

Coleman thought for a few more minutes, trying to piece together the facts of the crime with his suppositions.

"He's going to do what Cooper never had the guts to do—expose himself for who he truly is."

*But how?*

Coleman stared at the board for another fifteen minutes without moving.

Then another thought hit him. He called up the FBI offices again. However, he'd filled up Banks' voicemail so that the phone system returned him to an automated operator. Instead of giving up, he decided to spell Jones' name on the directory tree and see if he could reach him instead.

"This is Agent Jones."

"Agent Jones, this is Harold Coleman."

Coleman could almost imagine Jones' eye roll.

"What do *you* want, Mr. Coleman?"

"I want you to connect me with Agent Banks. I've been trying to reach her all day."

"She's probably avoiding you. Are you aware that we can get a restraining order against you if you keep this up?"

"I need to talk with her."

"To be honest, sir, I haven't seen her since early this morning."

"Did she check out Gordon's alibi?"

"Yep. And he passed with flying colors. Said he was at a bar last night with some friends—and it all checked out. We even saw pictures of him with his friends."

"But—"

"There are some things that are difficult to fake, Mr. Coleman, even in this day and age."

"But you don't know where she is?"

"Please, go enjoy your retirement in peace. We'll handle everything from here. We're not going to stop until we catch the bastard who's done this."

"I'm afraid you're—"

"Good-bye, Mr. Coleman."

*Click.*

Coleman seethed as he slammed his phone down.

"Is everything okay down there, Harold?" Edith called from upstairs.

"Just peachy, dear."

He picked up the phone book on the edge of his desk and thumbed through the pages.

*Something's not right.*

He punched in the numbers and waited.

"Northwest Aerial Services. This is Tommy," answered the voice on the other end.

"Tommy? Tommy Spurlock?" Coleman asked.

"Yes? Who's this?"

"I'm Harold Coleman and I'm looking for a couple of friends of mine. And I've got a feeling you might know where they are."

"Who is this again?"

"Harold Coleman—I know Carlton Gordon has been using your planes. He didn't happen to stop by today, did he?"

"I'm not at liberty to disclose—"

"Cut the crap, Tommy. Did you or did you not fly them today?"

Spurlock cleared his throat. "Well, since you're not currently in law enforcement, I guess it's okay to tell you that I did."

"And where are they now?"

"They all jumped."

"*All?*"

"Yes, Agent Banks, Mr. Flynn and Carlton Gordon."

"And where did they jump?"

"Hold on a second. Let me get the coordinates."

A few minutes later, Coleman grabbed a few things out of the basement and stuffed them into a small backpack and stomped upstairs.

"Going somewhere, Harold?" Edith asked as he reached the top of the stairs.

"I've got to go check on the car—make sure the paint matches."

"You don't need me to go with you?"

"Not this time. I'll be back soon, but go ahead and eat without me. Never know what trouble I might run into out there."

"Well, don't go looking for trouble, Harold. It seems to find you on its own easily enough."

He climbed into Edith's car and turned the ignition. The car's engine came alive, but he kept it in park. Quickly, he dialed Jones' direct line.

Voicemail.

"Agent Jones," he said after the beep. "I know where Agent Banks is—and Mr. Flynn, too."

# CHAPTER 37

FLYNN TURNED AROUND SLOWLY and grabbed Banks' arm. He held up his forefinger and mouthed, "Don't move," to her. He eyed the black bear lumbering toward him.

"I want you to slowly walk backward," he whispered in Banks' ear.

"What is it?" she asked.

"A black bear—but don't panic."

Flynn kept his eyes locked on the bear, who stopped and raised up on its hind legs, sniffing.

*Think, Flynn. Think.*

It wasn't enough that he'd just been hurled toward the earth without a parachute and managed to survive—and a crazy man was soon coming after him. But now he had to deal with a bear.

The bear snorted again and took several more steps in his direction before stopping.

Flynn went over the options in his mind, none of which assured him a positive outcome.

They could run, but black bears were fast. And while he might outrun Banks, they both wouldn't survive, which was the goal.

They could swim, but black bears were good swimmers, contrary to popular belief. He considered the thought of getting caught in the water by a black bear for a moment—and considered other options.

They could climb a tree, but black bears were actually better climbers than other bears and would likely catch them before they reached a height that the bear would balk at.

Finally, they could play dead—a tactic that works great with grizzlies but not with black bears.

*We're screwed.*

He said a little prayer under his breath, as it was the only option that presented a ray of hope.

Then a thought hit him.

*It's our clothes.*

He inched backward while watching the black bear stand on its hind legs, sniffing the air. Flynn glanced over his shoulder at Banks.

"Strip!" he whispered.

"What?"

"I said, 'Strip!' "

"Are you crazy? It's snowing!"

"So you want to be warm as this bear rips you limb from limb. Strip!"

As Flynn continued to move backward, he took his shoes off so he could drop his pants. He ripped his sweatshirt off and unbuttoned his shirt as quickly as possible.

"Why are we doing this again?" Banks asked.

"Cheap thrills?" Flynn shot back.

"This isn't a time for joking around."

Flynn jammed his foot back into his shoes and kept edging backward. "That bastard Gordon rubbed raw meat all over us. We smell like a steak to him."

He looked over his shoulder at Banks.

"Eyes forward," she said.

Flynn held out his hand and Banks understood. She placed her clothes in them—and he tossed them toward the pile of his clothes a few feet in front of him.

"Think this is gonna work?" she asked.

"I wish I could instill more confidence in you, but this is our only option. If it doesn't work, we're dinner tonight for that guy—at least one of us is."

"Good thing I won the state in the one hundred meters," she quipped.

"And I won the title of rock wall climbing champion for the Southeast Region when I was 18," he snapped back. "Looks like it's going to be a roll of the dice if this idea doesn't work."

"Chivalry is truly dead," she said.

They both continued to creep backward as they watched the bear near their clothes. He shoved his snout toward the pile and started to sniff. Reaching down with his paws, he picked it up and took a bite. Flynn's designer jeans were quickly shredded in front of him, but he didn't flinch.

*At least it wasn't my leg.*

Flynn held his arm up and motioned for her to move quickly. "Go, go!"

He turned and started to run with her. After about fifty yards, he looked back over his shoulder and saw the silhouette of the bear still standing where it had been before, ripping at the clothes.

That was the last time Flynn turned around.

"Keep going," he said, urging Banks forward.

Stripped down to their underwear with nothing else other than their shoes, they both raced through the woods, dodging the thick undergrowth as the snow began to pick up.

After a few minutes of hard running, Banks finally spoke.

"So, we're not going to get eaten by a bear, but we are going to freeze to death," she said.

Flynn knew she was right. If they didn't get somewhere warm quickly, they faced a night with nothing more than a flicker of hope for a sunrise. But he refused to let such negative talk distract him from their task.

"Let's keep going as far as we can—Gordon won't be far behind," Flynn said.

"Or he might be in our way, up ahead," she said.

"How would he know that?"

"Maybe he put some GPS tracking on us?"

"Good thing we stripped then."

She glanced at him. "If you suggest we go skinny dipping now, I'm going to slug you."

"Just keep going. There's got to be something up ahead here in the woods."

Several minutes later, Flynn tripped on a stump, sending him tumbling to the ground. Blood streaked down his neck as he rolled over and stood up.

A gunshot echoed in the woods, scattering birds and disturbing the otherwise peaceful night.

"That can't be good," Banks said as she scanned the tree canopy.

"Hunting season is pretty much over, except for cougars," Flynn said.

"Like I said, it can't be good."

Flynn sat up and dusted the snow off of him. "Fortunately, I'm still good," he said as he looked around. "Well, other than the fact that I'm in my underwear, I'm cold as hell, and there's a mad man chasing us through the woods with a gun after he threw us out of a plane." He froze and turned his attention to the distance. "Is that what I think it is?"

"What? What do you see?" she said.

He pointed west. "Over there. Is that a cabin, with lights on?"

"I think you're right," Banks said.

She helped him to his feet.

Almost immediately, Flynn put his head down and started running.

Hope had grown to more than a flicker.

# CHAPTER 38

GORDON WATCHED THE LIFE leak out of the black bear in front of him, a stream of crimson hue darkening the snow. He never intended to kill anyone—not even an animal. But when his original plans went awry, he was forced to make some changes. D.B. Cooper was no killer—and neither was he. But pressure can always change things. And he was changing in front of his own eyes.

After a few minutes, the bear went limp, a pair of pants hanging out of its mouth. Gordon would've preferred to see at least one human carcass strewn about the forest floor, two if he were lucky. However, the lack of blood indicated Banks and Flynn were long gone—and they had to be dealt with. They'd outsmarted him in the interim, but he doubted running naked through the woods in the snow would result in their eventual escape.

He took a deep breath and surveyed the landscape. With the snow starting to come down furiously, he needed to hustle if he was going to take advantage of their bold footprints.

Yet despite his urge to move quickly, he couldn't help but wonder what Cooper felt like as he drifted down among these same thick woods more than forty years ago. Was he scared? Was he excited? Did he experience an unmatched level of exhilaration? Gordon already experienced the pulse-pounding excitement of getting away with a crime and returning home as if he had just gone out for groceries or picked up his dry cleaning. But now he was on location, seeing the woods as perhaps Cooper did.

Only this time, Gordon was the one doing the man-hunting with an FBI agent on the run.

He stomped along, following the two pair of diminishing human footprints. The gusting wind and the airy snow proved to be uncooperative as he tracked them. At one point, he traveled fifty meters down a trail before realizing they weren't his fugitives' tracks. He returned to the fork in the path and saw that what he originally took as human footprints were boot prints. But his mistake alerted him to the fact that he wasn't alone in the woods.

An owl hooted overhead and leaves rustled behind him, causing Gordon to spin around. Instead of catching his prey, he watched a deer bound off down the trail.

Since he first hit the ground, the temperature had steadily dropped. By now, he guessed it was no warmer than twenty when he factored in the wind. He stopped and took off his gloves, digging in his coat pocket for his pack of Raleighs.

He'd quit smoking several years ago after the constant nagging from his doctor—and he had to ask why. He traded *potential* lung cancer for stage four stomach cancer, at least that's how he viewed it.

With the cigarette resting gingerly on his lips, he cupped one hand and struck the match with the other, shielding it from the wind. He held the small flame to the end of the cigarette and sucked in a long breath. The nicotine infused smoke rushed into his lungs, the smell of smoldering tobacco saturating the air around him. It was far from the best cigarette he'd ever had, but this was more than about taking a drag. It was about experiencing everything as Cooper did.

Gordon put his gloves back on and continued to follow the footprints. It was only a matter of time before he bagged his prey.

# CHAPTER 39

COLEMAN ROARED SOUTH down I-5 toward his intended destination. What was normally a picturesque drive on a clear day turned into a painful venture down memory lane. He was going to put the past where it belonged and leave it buried there. But it had a way of resisting any such final pronouncements.

For the past decade, the whispers and stares subsided. Time—along with a sweeping tide of wrinkles in combination with a disappearing hairline—provided the necessary distance he needed to escape the gawkers and the gossipers in public. Whether real or imagined, he spent years as a tormented and failed FBI agent. It didn't help that the public actually rooted for the bad guy.

*At least they picked the right side this time.*

The rise of social media led to this criminal—Who was he kidding? It was definitely Carlton Gordon—being the one mocked and ridiculed as failed and desperate. Yet, the fact that Gordon had stolen $1.2 million from the U.S. government didn't make him appear such a failure to Coleman. Forget the fact that he hardly kept a dime of it. Just the idea that he could get away with such a brazen act and never suffer a single consequence grated on Coleman's last nerve.

He'd lost count of all the times television crews interviewed him for documentaries and programs about D.B. Cooper. Even more annoying in recent years were the suggestions that a man named Kenny Christensen was indeed D.B. Cooper, and he had ignored all the signs that pointed to this obvious suspect. Just when he thought he'd disappear into relative obscurity, these shows came at him fast and furious—and if he didn't need the money, he would've told them all to go to hell.

In a way, the ridicule was his own fault, a byproduct of his greed. If he'd just politely declined, nobody in Seattle or the rest of the United States would have known what he looked like. But now his face was out there for everyone to see. And every few years, on a certain milestone anniversary, they replayed his interviews.

If Edith ever caught him watching one of the programs, she'd snatch the remote out of his hand and turn off the television. "It's in the past, Harold. Forgive yourself and forget about it," she would tell him every time. Her disdain for those interviews was only surpassed by Coleman's inability to look away from them.

Yet as he drove down I-5, he replayed every single interview in his head, especially the one where he stated it was highly unlikely that Cooper survived the jump. When asked why a body was never found—or even any money beyond $5,000 buried near a sandbar—Coleman answered, "Have you ever been in those woods? Just go spend a few days down there and see if you think a man running around in a suit would last more than twenty-four hours without getting caught by either a person or a wild animal."

Coleman spent more hours in those woods than he

cared to, far more than he could count. At one point in the days immediately following Cooper's heist, Coleman cornered a man that matched Cooper's description, only to find out it was a mentally ill man who couldn't form complete sentences—and he had an airtight alibi. Even more embarrassing was the fact that someone in the search party leaked the story to the press.

However, none of his failures as lead investigator in the case were as damaging to his reputation as they were to his career opportunities. Before this debacle, he'd closed more than ninety-five percent of his cases, drawing high praise from his superiors. The whispers around him said he was in line to become chief of the field office, perhaps even more if he relocated to D.C. And it certainly looked promising—until D.B. Cooper jumped out of a plane with $200,000.

As Coleman jammed his foot on the gas, he knew the consequences of his impending actions.

*It's now or never.*

Everything else was lost, gone forever. But his good name and reputation? He held out hope he could reclaim it.

He pulled into the gravel parking lot along the banks of Lake Merwin. Based off what Tommy Spurlock had told him, he was sure to find Banks and Flynn in this area being pursued by Gordon.

Climbing out of his car, he zipped his jacket up tight, unfolded his walking stick, and fished his flashlight out of his pocket. He stopped for a moment, placing his light on the ground, and dug in his jacket pocket. Before he took another step, he needed to make sure he was prepared, ready to confront the slippery thief.

She was there all right—his gun. He pressed the palm of his hand against the cold steel. A smile spread across his face.

He was ready for whatever happened next.

## CHAPTER 40

WHEN FLYNN AND BANKS reached the front of the cabin, they both paused before walking up the steps. Flynn knew how it looked—and it looked scandalous at best. A man and a woman, both scantily clad, prancing through the snowy forest. An affair gone wrong? Perhaps. Almost any lie they told was far more believable than the truth.

Flynn smiled to himself as he thought about how the truth might sound. "Excuse me, sir. We were wondering if you could help us. The two of us were thrown from an airplane with only one parachute. After we somehow survived, we came across a bear who would've eaten us had we not stripped down to our underwear. We've traveled at least five miles in the freezing wind and snow and were wondering if you could provide us some assistance, starting with a warm meal and some warmer clothing?"

This wasn't exactly going to swing open doors—not to mention people who lived this far out in the sticks did so to get away from people.

Banks tried to cover herself as she shivered. "Well, what are you waiting for?" she said as they stood on the steps.

Flynn stepped forward and knocked.

For a few moments, not a sound escaped from the cabin.

"Someone's gotta be here," she said. "If not, we're

commandeering the place—official FBI business."

"You can still do that?"

"I'd rather seek an apology than permission. And even if I wanted to do the latter, I couldn't exactly do that right now, could I?"

Flynn smiled and shook his head.

Still nothing.

"Knock again," she said.

He held his hand up. "Just chill out."

"No pun intended?"

"Seriously, banging on a guy's cabin in the woods in the middle of the night is how you wind up dead."

"Frostbite will get you, too."

Flynn raised his clenched fist to rap on the door again when he heard shuffling across the wooden floor. He cut his eyes at Banks. "See. Just be patient."

A shadow passed in front of the small glass opening on the door, veiled by a thin swath of cloth. When a hand pulled back the curtain, a large bearded face appeared, startling both Flynn and Banks.

"What do you want?" the man asked, the tip of his shotgun peeking up just above the bottom of the window.

"We're freezing and we need your help," Flynn said.

The man looked Flynn and Banks up and down. "Not too many people go skinny dipping this time of year."

"Please, sir," Banks said. "We didn't go skinny dipping. We had to strip to avoid a bear."

The man grunted and showed a hint of a smile. "If I had a nickel for every couple that said that when they appeared on my doorstep in the middle of the night—"

He released the curtain and unlocked the door, obviously satisfied that they posed him no threat.

With his thick hands, he waved them inside. "Come on in."

Flynn and Banks rushed inside, barely waiting for the invitation. They headed directly toward the roaring fire in the stone fireplace located in the center of the room.

"Can I get you a blanket and a hot cup of cocoa?" the man asked.

"That'd be great," Banks said.

"You?" he asked, looking at Flynn.

"Yes, please," Flynn said.

He lit a match and twisted the stove burner until the gas caught the flame, bringing the burner to life. He shook out the match and filled up a kettle with water.

"So, what are you two really doing out here?" he asked.

"I'm an FBI agent," Banks said. "And we're being pursued by a suspect."

The man stopped. "Now, hold up. *You* are being pursued by a suspect? I've been livin' in these woods a long time, but even that seems a little backward to me."

Flynn shook his head. "You're right. It is backward. But it's the truth."

The man laughed. "I hardly believe any government person when they say it's the truth."

Flynn held up both hands, gesturing surrender. "I'm not a government type, please."

The man cocked his head and eyed Flynn closely. "Wait a minute. I've seen you before. You're that conspiracy nut I see on television all the time."

Flynn opened his mouth to assuage the man's fears that he was a nut before he continued.

"I'm a big fan of your work," he said, offering his hand to Flynn. "Mark Justice."

"James Flynn," he said as they shook hands. "And that's Agent Jennifer Banks."

Justice hustled across the room and shook Banks' hand before grabbing a blanket off the back of the couch and giving it to her.

"So, what were you two really up to tonight? Some kinda special stake out?" Justice said before flashing them a wink. He paused. "Never mind. It's none of my business. Live and let live. You two are grown consenting adults. But let me get you some clothes."

Flynn glanced around at the cabin. His instinct drew him to pictures, anything to give him a sense of what kind of man Mark Justice was. But other than a few pictures of him squatting beside a dead elk, the walls were barren.

Most of the furniture appeared handmade, rough-hewn from timber felled in the nearby woods and shaped into adequate tables, chairs, and couches. No television or computer. A beat up radio occupied a spot atop his refrigerator next to a box of cigarettes.

Then he froze.

His eyes scanned back toward the fridge.

*Is that what I think it is?*

He nudged Banks with his elbow and pointed with his nose. Her eyes widened. "No way!" she muttered.

The kettle started to whistle, drawing Justice back into the room. "I got it," he said, removing the kettle from the burner.

He spun around and tossed each of them warm clothes. For Banks, he had a pair of sweatpants and a hooded sweatshirt. For Flynn, an old pair of jeans and a long-sleeve flannel shirt.

"One of you can grab that old jacket up there on the coat rack when you leave," Justice said. "It's my daughter's and she hasn't been out here to visit for at least fifteen years."

"I'm sorry to hear that," Banks said.

He waved her off. "Awww, it's no big deal. That's life. We make decisions and live with the consequences. I've got not reason to be sentimental over it. It's just a jacket."

Flynn nodded. "So, how long have you been living out here?"

Justice shrugged. "Quite a while—so long, I've lost count."

"I'm always curious what draws people to live secluded like this. What drew you to the woods?" Flynn asked.

"A fresh start, I guess. Seattle was gettin' too big for me—and I liked the outdoors. This seemed like a great place to settle down."

"Wow," Flynn said. "What kind of work were you in?"

Justice stopped and took a deep breath. "A bunch of things, really. I'd get bored with one thing and move on to another—but I still managed to pay my bills."

"Like what kind of things?"

"You sure are nosy, Mr. Flynn. I've seen people ask you questions, but I didn't know you could dish it out as well."

Flynn's eyes narrowed as he turned his head to one side and pointed toward the living room. "Now, you said you don't have a television, but you're familiar with my work?"

"Got a TV in my room—and all your books on my shelf right here." Justice shuffled across the room toward a large bookshelf. He knocked on the side of it. "Made this

bookshelf myself—one of the many jobs I ventured into."
He paused. "Now, let's see. Where is that one?" After a few
seconds, "Ah-ha! Here it is, *Cooper's Coup: How D.B. Cooper
Confounded the FBI and Vanished with Federal Money*. It's one of
my favorites. Would you mind signing it for me?"

Flynn's face lit up, while Banks rolled her eyes.

"You're just feeding his ego, you know?" she quipped.

Justice ignored her while he rummaged through a
kitchen drawer for a black pen. "Found one! Here you go."
He handed the pen to Flynn.

"Excellent," Flynn said as he scribbled his autograph
onto the first title page in the book."

Justice took it from him and looked at it, his brow furrowed. "Really? Just your name? How about something like,
'To Mark, the greatest hermit there ever was'?"

"Well, we just met—and I know quite a few hermits—
mostly authors, of course," Flynn said, taking the book back.
"But I think I can justify that caveat." He scribbled the note out
above his autograph and handed it back to Justice. Flynn glanced
at the cigarettes on top of the fridge, catching Justice's eye.

"You smoke?" Justice asked.

Flynn shook his head. "Not very often—and mostly
cigars when I do." He paused. "Certainly not forty-year-old
cigarettes."

"Ha! These are the best damn cigarettes you'll ever put
in your mouth."

"Even after all those years?"

Justice rubbed his face with both hands and took a sip
of his cocoa. "What are you? A cigarette historian?"

"No, I just—"

"He's just obsessed with Raleigh cigarettes," Banks interrupted. "His grandma used to smoke them—sentimental value. You know how it goes."

"My grandmother used to smoke them, too," Justice said. "She died of lung cancer. They never could figure out what caused it."

Unsure if he was deadpanning or serious, Flynn started to say something, but Banks put her index finger on her lips and gave him a knowing look.

After a few more minutes of small talk, Justice asked them if they wanted refills. They both declined.

"Well, I'm glad I could help you out—and wish I could help you more," Justice said, "but I've got to get to bed."

"Can we call someone and wait for them to pick us up?" Banks said. "I can make sure you're compensated."

"No offense, ma'am, but I don't need compensation, but I do need sleep. Unfortunately, I don't have a phone. Luckily for you, you now have all you need to brave the elements and find your way back to civilization," he said, pressing a flashlight into her hand. "Take this and you'll be fine."

"I'm not sure this is a good idea," Flynn said.

Justice walked up to Flynn and stood inches away from him. "Well, I am. The last thing I want is someone wandering around my property in the middle of the night. I'm liable to shoot them in the head, which will cause a big fuss, and might end up in me getting a prison sentence. And quite frankly, I'd rather just go to bed and bypass all that." He paused. "Just follow the shoreline for about eight miles and you'll be just fine. There are plenty of folks who live around a state park area there that would surely help you."

"You sure that's wise. We might be able to see more easily, but so will this lunatic chasing us," Banks protested.

"Exactly," Justice said. "It is easier to see, but it also improves your chances of surviving out here tonight until you can reach help."

"Are you sure we can't stay here tonight?" Banks asked again.

He nodded. "I'm sure. Now run along. If you go about a quarter of a mile west, you'll eventually weave your way down the embankment toward the water. From there on out, it's cake."

"Thank you," Flynn said as he nodded.

"Oh, and Mr. Flynn?"

"Yes?"

Justice lumbered down the steps. "Mind if I have my mug before you go? I have no idea why you'd take it, but I'm gonna need that back."

Flynn acted surprised and forced a laugh. "I'm not sure why this was in my hand—probably because you were such a hospitable host."

"Never been called that before," Justice mumbled. "Well, good luck in your journey."

"Thanks," Banks said. "Same to you."

With that, they headed down the path Justice directed them to. They hadn't gone more than fifty yards before a coyote howled in the distance.

"You think that was—"

"Nah," Banks said. "But nice attempt at trying to get his DNA with his coffee cup. You almost pulled it off."

"You know what I always say—why just solve one crime when you can solve two?"

A gunshot crackled through the air.

"Keep moving," Banks said. "I'm sure we'll be out of here soon enough."

# CHAPTER 41

GORDON SLOGGED THROUGH THE SNOW, which turned heavy and wet on his feet. He hadn't noticed any shoes when he came across the bear. It was too late to lament his failure to slather Flynn and Banks' shoes in raw meat too.

*You live, you learn.*

He stopped and put his hand on the pine tree just off the path. The pain in Gordon's stomach sharpened, drawing a wince from him. After a few moments, the pain subsided and he continued to track his two fugitives streaking through the woods.

During hunting trips with his father, Gordon learned plenty of things about life—and a few things about tracking your prey. "Never let them see you coming," his father told him one night around the campfire. It proved to be the exact advice he needed the next morning. Gordon spotted an elk and tracked him for several miles with the help of his father. Eventually, the animal backed itself into a corner, seemingly unaware that he was being followed. Gordon snuck around and positioned himself behind a boulder. When the elk turned and looked in his direction, he was unaware he'd already sighted in on a rifle scope by a hunter. With the collectedness of a veteran hunter, Gordon pulled the trigger.

But instead of watching the animal collapse onto the ground, it bounded away. He'd missed from a short distance—no more than fifty yards—and his father never let him live it down.

"The yips will ruin your life," Gordon's father told him. "If you can't pull the trigger when your goal is in sight, you're going to always play second fiddle to someone. And life behaves like an elk—you hardly ever get a second chance once you miss."

It was the seminal event that drove Gordon, motivating him to succeed in everything he did.

But here he was once again, trudging through the woods after a failed attempt. He never considered the possibility that he would actually have to kill someone—it's why he hoped nature would do the job for him. A brutal winter storm, a bear, a fall. Nature and the elements were on his side, creating difficult survival odds for his prey. Not to mention the unfamiliar terrain at the beginning of a storm. However, for Gordon, this was familiar territory.

After he missed the elk, his father made him track it down again for a second shot. "We're not leaving this mountain until you kill that bull," his father said. Then he went one step further. "You're not getting anything to eat until you shoot him."

Gordon watched the elk long enough that he figured out where it was going—and the route it wanted to take. With deft skill and speed, Gordon navigated through a mountainside of craggy rocks in order to take up a position in front of the elk. After lying in wait for over an hour, Gordon watched the elk wander right into his path. This time, he didn't miss, felling the beast on the spot.

"Why couldn't you have done this when there was far more daylight?" his father groused as he dressed the elk in the field.

Gordon watched his father's every move as the knife sawed through the tendons and ligaments of the once-regal creature. Now a bloody mess enveloped the mutilated carcass on the snow. Just before dark, his father finished dressing the elk and they hauled it back to their campsite under the pale moonlight.

"Next time, don't miss on your first shot," Gordon's father said.

The words echoed in Gordon's ears as he neared a darkened cabin in the woods. Flynn and Banks' tracks led him to this point, though it was unlikely that they were still there.

Gordon settled behind a rock and pulled out his binoculars. He peered through them, hoping to catch a glimpse of either of them. Nothing. Just an elderly man reading a book in front of a roaring fire. It looked warm and inviting—but the man didn't. Gordon feared that if he approached the cabin, he might find himself in an unwelcome gunfight. While he'd scouted this area for years, he didn't know the man who owned the home. But he knew that an unwelcome visitor might draw out the man—with his gun. Not to mention, it might also get him recognized. If he could take care of business sooner rather than later, he might avoid being seen. But that was a big *if*, yet it was a risk worth taking as opposed to tangling with a mountain man, who appeared comfortable and content to sit in his chair and read. Smoke billowed from the chimney, but Gordon detected no other signs of life. If Flynn and Banks had indeed visited this cabin, they were gone by now—and had been so for hours.

He edged close enough to the house to identify the exit path Flynn and Banks took. With his flashlight trained on the ground, Gordon moved along, hoping not to disturb the man who appeared frozen and rigid as he read a book in his living room.

The snow continued to pelt him, eventually increasing in its intensity. He had to keep moving—and moving quickly. If he didn't, the trail would go cold, swallowed up by the fresh snow.

Gordon hustled along for more than half an hour. He didn't need to stop for breaks. Adrenaline coursed through his veins. His prey couldn't be far away.

Then he froze, straining to hear with his right ear. The voices of two people talking could be heard up ahead. A wry smile leaked across his face.

He continued tracking the footprints for several minutes until the voices grew louder. And in the darkness, he strained to see the silhouettes of a man and a woman.

Flynn and Banks.

He knelt down and pulled his binoculars out of his backpack, utilizing the night vision option as he studied them through the glass. There was no denying it was them.

He set aside his binoculars and rubbed his hands together.

*It won't be long now. You're all mine.*

# CHAPTER 42

FLYNN AND BANKS SCRAMBLED up and down the mountainous terrain. Outfitted by Mark Justice, they had sufficient clothing to brave the elements. While they both agreed it wasn't ideal, the thought of being hunkered down in a cabin and dependent upon Justice to defend them felt like a big gamble. Flynn argued that at least out in the elements they could use their training to survive, if not capture Gordon.

Banks took the lead, keeping her flashlight trained on the ground and alerting Flynn to any major obstacles along the path.

"You know this guy is going to kill us if he finds us," she said over her shoulder.

Flynn grunted. "I wouldn't be so sure."

"This is all for his jollies—the sick bastard."

"Perhaps, but his jollies have given us a chance to flip the script on him. If we get out of this mess, he's going to be the one running."

"And I'm sure he's already got a golden parachute waiting, no pun intended."

Flynn stumbled over a root but avoided tumbling to the dirt. "Give me a heads up back here."

"Sorry. I must've stepped right over it and missed it."

"Anyway, if Gordon's got an escape plan, he's not going to act on it until we're out of the way. He's banking on us not being able to let anyone know what's going on until it's too late. I'm sure he scouted out this area before he dumped us here. He's been meticulous and two steps ahead of us at every turn."

Banks slowed down and stopped in the middle of the trail. "I need to take a break." She pulled a bottle of water out of the small backpack Justice had given them and chugged half of it before handing it to Flynn.

Flynn looked behind them down the trail. He didn't see anything—and the only thing he heard was Banks' panting and an occasional owl hooting.

Banks took the bottle back from Flynn and shoved it into her pack. "You know what I don't get?"

"What?"

"How did Gordon have a legitimate alibi for each of the crimes? Somebody always talks."

Flynn shrugged. "Maybe he paid them well."

"But even money doesn't explain how he had pictures of himself at different locations during the exact moment of the crime."

"Pictures can be faked."

"I had forensics look at the files—they said they were legit."

He sighed. "Well, there's another possibility that we have yet to discuss about him."

"What's that?"

"That he's merely the mastermind behind the crimes and wasn't the one who committed them."

She shook her head. "But how does that account for

the mystery man with cigarettes wearing Stallion cologne?"

"Coincidence?"

"That would just be too coincidental—and I can't imagine Gordon and his accomplice would wear the same cologne."

"Does he have a twin? That could explain the same preference."

Banks chuckled. "What do you think this is? An episode of some mindless cop drama on network television?" She paused. "Besides, I already checked into that. There's no twin—not even a brother or a sister."

"Let's get movin' again," Flynn said. "I'd rather not ask him that question as an unarmed man."

She smiled and resumed her brisk pace along the path. "So what are we missing?"

"I'm not sure, but we're missing something. This guy hasn't been pulling the wool over our eyes on his own."

For the next two hours, Flynn and Banks continued on in relative silence. Only the occasional water break impeded their torrid pace.

"Eight miles? Isn't that what Justice said because this feels like at least ten," Banks grumbled.

"Perhaps he was dead on," Flynn said. "Isn't that a light I see up ahead there?"

"I think you're right. Through that clearing up ahead, I see somethin'. This has gotta be the state park he mentioned."

"It sure is," he said, running up next to her and pointing at a sign to their right. "Turn your light off."

Banks clicked the light off. "You think that's Gordon? Like he knew exactly where we were and was waiting for us?"

Flynn shrugged. "Could be. I'm beginning to wonder

if even Mark Justice wasn't planted there by him. That'd be a stroke of genius if it was."

"This is no time to admire the criminal," Banks whispered. "You got any ideas how we can tell if this is Gordon or not?"

Flynn crouched down near a sign before the woods gave way to a large clearing. Snow pelted them as the cold air joined the assault on their senses, mostly their extremities. A parking lot along with a boat ramp and a sandy beach area let them know they'd reached their destination. But without knowing who was in the car about a hundred yards away with its headlights on, they couldn't proceed.

"Just sit tight for a moment and see what happens," he said.

After about five minutes with no movement, Banks looked at Flynn. "This is ridiculous. That guy isn't getting out of his car. He's just—"

Banks' eyes widened. She didn't see the car door open, but she heard it slam. She whipped her head back toward the parking lot.

"Who's that?" she asked.

"Ssshhh," Flynn said, holding up his index finger.

"After a few seconds, a pair of feet hit the pavement along with a cane. The man pulled himself upright."

"Harold Coleman?" Banks said. "What is he doing out here?"

"There's only one way to find out," Flynn said, refusing to wait. He dashed out of the woods and into the parking lot toward him.

Banks ran up behind him and shined her light in his face. Coleman shielded his eyes from the light.

"Harold Coleman? Is that you?"

# CHAPTER 43

GORDON STOOPED OVER and rested his hands on his knees—and he never would've stopped unless he had to. The burning sensation in his stomach had spread to his back. He spit onto the ground, staining the powdery snow crimson. Slowly, he picked his head up and looked around. In all his scheming, he never imagined being unable to finish the job.

*Just keep moving.*

The adverse weather brought gusts of wind along with it, the kind that peeled the warmth right off a person's face. Gordon could feel his face starting to go numb.

"It wouldn't be fun if it wasn't a challenge," Gordon said aloud in a mocking tone.

At least, that's what his father used to tell him, though he never agreed. One day when Gordon was eleven, his father caught him shooting crows off the power line near their home with a rifle. His father grabbed him by the scruff of his neck and led him behind the shed in their backyard.

"Son, if I ever catch you shooting at a defenseless animal like this again, I swear I'm gonna beat you six ways from Sunday," he growled as he snatched the gun out of his hand. "Shooting is a sport—and it's not sporting if it's not fair."

Gordon watched in horror as his father loaded the gun and shot at his dog.

"Think that's fair?" he roared.

Through tear-stained eyes, Gordon rushed over to his golden retriever, Choco, who was cowering in the corner, unharmed by his father's attempt at a lesson.

"You didn't have to shoot at him," Gordon said while he hugged Choco.

His dad spit on the ground and put his hands on his hips. "I think I did," he snarled. "I made my point, didn't I?"

He stormed off and left Gordon sobbing.

That traumatic event forced Gordon to come to terms with his father's brutality. He never hit Gordon, but there was never any question of physical abuse. It was a hundred percent mental.

And it's exactly the same behavior he was emulating as he trudged ahead, pain and all, in pursuit of Flynn and Banks.

*Dad would be so proud.*

Or maybe he wouldn't. It certainly wasn't sporting to push two people out of an airplane with only one parachute. Nor was it fair to slather bloody raw meat on them before dropping them in bear country. And removing all chance of reaching the outside world without a long trek through unfamiliar mountainous terrain during an early season snowstorm wasn't exactly leveling the playing field either.

*Dad was wrong. This* is *fun.*

Gordon glanced down at the GPS in his hand. He could hear Flynn and Banks talking up ahead—and he could tell the state park recreational area was no more than five hundred yards ahead.

As he crept closer, he reverted to a stealthier approach, walking on his toes in an effort to reduce the sound of snow crunching beneath his feet. His movement toward them was a practice in patience and concentration. Moments away from flushing them into the open, Gordon didn't want to lose sight of them for a second, nor did he want to stumble along the trail and give up the element of surprise. Everything was at stake.

Nearly unflappable, Gordon gritted his teeth and pressed on.

Step. Step. Step.

He checked the snow-coated forest path in front of him before glancing in the direction of his prey.

Step. Step. Step.

Low murmurs helped him remain focused on the ground as he moved forward. As long as he knew they were still crouching in the woods, unwilling to dash into the open, he had them right where he wanted them.

Step. Step. Step.

Gordon looked down and then up again. But this time, the silhouetted figures he expected to be hiding just off the pathway at the entrance of the forest trail were gone.

*What the—*

Step. Step. Step.

He stopped caring as much about his stealthy approach when he realized they were gone. But he still didn't want to give up his position either.

After a few more meters, Gordon came upon the spot where Flynn and Banks had been hiding. He peered around a sign just off the pathway.

*There they are.*

He smiled to himself as he watched them try to talk to an old man about their situation and where they were. It was evident they were trying to talk him into helping them.

Gordon squinted, straining to see the man's face.

"Is that—?" He stopped talking to himself for a moment before resuming. "That can't be him. How'd he track me out here?"

Gordon stood up and hustled toward them.

*It's time to get down to business.*

He pulled back the hammer on his pistol as he approached them, drawing their attention away from Coleman.

"Who's ready to dance?" Gordon growled.

# CHAPTER 44

THE HEADLIGHTS GLINTED off Coleman's gun as he held it loosely by his side. Flynn noticed Coleman teeter as he stood in front of them. The man didn't say a word.

With both hands surrendered in the air, Flynn focused his gaze on Gordon. "I think you better put your gun down before you make a terrible mistake."

Gordon shuffled closer, edging within ten feet of the trio. "You've already made a terrible mistake—and it's going to cost you dearly. You see, Coleman and I have been working together this whole time. I knew no one would believe a maligned FBI agent, a man who deserved better. But you and every other agent in the Bureau treated him like a pariah. Well, now you're going to pay for your lack of respect."

Flynn glanced at Banks. Her slight headshake signaled that she didn't want to encourage him to do anything. Flynn ignored her. He put his hands on his hips and took a step forward.

"Well, I'm not buying it," Flynn declared emphatically. "The Harold Coleman I know is a man who spent his whole life in search of the truth. And from where I'm standing, it seems like he was right all along. But I doubt he came here tonight to rub my nose in that fact before he shoots me."

Flynn took another step toward Gordon.

"That's far enough," Gordon said as he extended his gun in Flynn's direction.

Flynn noticed Gordon grimacing in pain, almost hunched over, with his left hand draped across his midsection. Without hesitating, Flynn took another step.

"I said, that's far enough," Gordon said, taking a step backward.

Before Gordon could make another move, Flynn crouched down and exploded with a leg kick up toward Gordon's stomach. The sudden movement caught Gordon off guard and he didn't have an opportunity to defend himself. With a powerful blow, Flynn sent the suspect tumbling backward.

Meanwhile, Banks wielded her own roundhouse kick toward Coleman, who didn't respond like a frail old man. Remaining upright, he grabbed her leg and threw her. She landed on her feet and wasted no time in sprinting toward him, landing a vicious uppercut that stunned him. He regained his bearings and grabbed her, throwing her to the ground. Pinning her arms down with his knees, he placed both hands around Banks' neck and started to choke her. Banks wrestled one arm free and tried to gouge him in the eye. He withdrew and avoided her attempt. Frantically searching for a way to extend the fight and give herself a chance to emerge victorious, she slapped the ground for something to assist her and put her hand on a rock. She swung hard at him, connecting with the side of his face when an odd thing happened—she slashed his face but no blood came out initially.

As they struggled, a mask fell off his face—and she realized that she wasn't fighting Coleman after all. It was her partner, Chase Jones.

"Jones!" she screamed. "I'm gonna kill you." In an adrenaline-induced rage, she squirmed free and kicked him in the face several times, rendering him incapacitated.

Banks snatched Jones' gun and stood up straight. She looked over at Flynn who had yet to get Gordon in a compromising position. Gordon kept his gun trained on Flynn.

"Well, well, well, I guess the secret is out of the bag," Gordon said as he broke into a guffaw. "Makes no difference to me. The outcome tonight will be no different—and the public will be none the wiser."

Banks saw Jones moving before she grabbed his arm and kicked him in the back. He fell face first in front of her. "So, it's games you like?" She didn't wait for a response. "This is one you can't win."

Gordon laughed again and shook his head. "Agent Banks, the woman with all the answers. Why don't you pull the trigger and get this over with? Or should I say, get this started? Because the second you pull that trigger, you're dead—and so is your partner. Because this time I won't miss."

Banks put her knee into Jones' back and leaned down toward his ear. "How could you? My own partner—a traitor. And with *him*, no less." She ripped what was left of his latex mask off his face and tossed it aside.

"I had no choice," Jones said. "He's blackmailing me. He kidnapped my son."

Banks put more weight on his back with her knee. "I've been working with you long enough to know when you're lying."

"I swear, it's true!" Jones said.

"Shut the hell up, Jones," Gordon said. "We met at a bar when you were drunk and you said you needed some money—all those gambling debts. And I offered you a solution. Simple as that."

"I should let her kill you right now," Jones said.

Gordon smiled. "First of all, she couldn't even if she wanted to. Secondly, if you do, you'll never find out where your share of the money is."

Jones squirmed, his chest still planted firmly against the ground. "I already know where it is—littered over CenturyLink Field."

"That's not all of it," Gordon said. "Besides, there's still room for you to emerge the hero of this story as long as you keep your head."

Flynn broke his silence. "The hero? He's going to prison when this is all over with, if not for collusion, most definitely for murder."

"Not after he arrests the Cooper Copycat and hauls him off to prison," Gordon said.

"You're a pathetic excuse for a copycat," Banks said.

"And you're a pathetic excuse for an FBI agent," Gordon shot back. "It took a retired disgraced agent to actually figure out who was behind everything—and you still didn't believe him. But I've managed to do everything Cooper did—and more."

Flynn broke into a quiet snicker.

"Something funny, hack?" Gordon said.

"Except you didn't outsmart the FBI," Flynn said. "They're going to cart you away to prison—and you'll never see the light of day again."

"You can dream, Mr. Flynn," Gordon said. "But it'll

never happen. I'll never be tried or convicted of anything, regardless of what transpires here tonight—that much I'm sure of."

"Then your arrogance will be your downfall," Banks chimed in.

"And your ignorance will be yours," Gordon said, training his gun on Banks. "I suggest you don't move another muscle or you'll be nothing more than a fallen agent who failed to capture another D.B. Cooper."

After a brief tense moment, Flynn spoke up. "So, I'll play along. How is Jones going to be the hero of this story?"

"Once I shoot you two and feed your bodies to the bears, Jones will arrest me. He'll be famous and make off with some of the loot. And I'll be famous as well. It's a win-win."

"Except you're going to prison," Flynn said.

Gordon started coughing and spewed a stream of blood onto the ground. He held up his finger and bent over while keeping an eye—and his gun—trained on Banks. "That's where you're wrong."

After another brief coughing spell, Gordon stood upright.

"I'm going to die, Agent Banks," he said. "I've got stomach cancer—and even if you shoot me now, you're only escalating the inevitable by a few weeks."

"But why?" Banks said. "What would compel you to do such a thing?"

"I do it for the same reason D.B. Cooper did all those years ago—because I can," Gordon said with a wry grin on his face. "The greatest American bandit in modern day history. He stumped the FBI and they never caught him—and if you arrest me, at least everyone will know who I really am. And it will come out that the only reason you figured out it was me was because I let you figure it out. You're ignorant *and* arrogant."

"And *you* are naive if you think anyone is ever going to celebrate you with songs and talk about you in pop culture," Flynn said. "You're nothing more than a sad wannabe."

Gordon shrugged. "Perhaps not, but at least I know what it's like to be D.B. Cooper. And at least my name won't go down in history as a failure."

The foursome was so engrossed in the conversation that no one heard the approaching footsteps—or the click of a gun.

# CHAPTER 45

"CUTE STORY, BUT IT ENDS RIGHT HERE," boomed a voice a few yards away from the foursome. Harold Coleman smiled as he lumbered forward, leaning on his walking stick with one hand and clutching his gun in the other.

"If I wasn't holding a gun, I'd slow clap for you right now," Gordon said. "It's about time you figured out what was going on."

"I've had you figured out all along, you sonofabitch. Nobody would believe me, but I'm hoping all the knuckleheads at the FBI will appreciate the fact that I stuck with this case, especially you, Agent Banks."

She forced a smile and nodded.

Gordon spit again onto the ground and grunted. "This isn't going to end like you think it is, *Agent* Coleman. Just another swing and a miss at trying to catch a fugitive criminal in the Washington mountains. I never thought you'd take it this far but I'm afraid you're going to be joining Mr. Flynn and Agent Banks on the dinner table of a few black bears."

"What's stopping me from shooting you right now? You think I give a damn?" Coleman growled.

Gordon shifted his weight from one foot to the other. "Oh, plenty is stopping you—you want to be the hero. You let D.B. Cooper slip away in these same woods but now you want to bring me in to redeem yourself—in your own mind, anyway. You'll always be the guy who failed the FBI."

With everyone engrossed in the conversation, Jones exploded off the ground, catching Banks by surprise and knocking her gun to the side. Jones scrambled for the gun and reached it before Banks. He then shot Coleman in the shoulder, sending him sprawling backward.

As Coleman fell, he dropped his gun. Flynn dove for it, but Gordon beat him to it, kicking it to the side. Flynn lunged for it again but froze when Gordon shot the ground, just inches away from him.

Gordon chuckled. "Seems like the odds have changed in my favor, thanks to another failed FBI agent trying to be a hero."

He paced around for a few moments before speaking again.

"We're going to do things my way, Mr. Flynn," Gordon said.

Coleman watched as Jones took full control of Banks, pinning her to the ground in the same manner as she held him only a few moments before. "I finished first in my class at Quantico, not second," Jones said as he applied more pressure on Banks' back.

Coleman lay back on the ground, trying to ignore the fiery pain consuming his right arm and the entire right side of his body. He put his left hand over the wound and applied pressure, trying to stop the bleeding.

*I'm this close to bringing this bastard in—I'm not going out like this.*

He glared at Gordon, who directed Flynn and Banks back toward the woods. Gordon and Jones flanked them, keeping their guns trained on the two hostages.

"You're just gonna leave me here to die?" Coleman said as he tried to stagger to his feet.

Coleman managed to get to his knees and was about to stand up before Gordon crept next to him and got in his ear.

"Yes, old man, you're going to die out here—alone— a failure," Gordon said. He cackled as he stood up and started to return toward his prisoners.

Coleman mustered up all his strength and hustled after Gordon.

"What the—" Gordon said as he spun around behind him, just in time to see Coleman's walking stick crash against his face.

Banks sprang into action against Jones, delivering a devastating wheelhouse kick to his side that knocked him off balance. Her second kick connected with his head, putting him out cold.

Meanwhile, Flynn picked up a rock and looked to finish the job Coleman started. He bashed Gordon in the head with it, stunning him for a moment. Gordon's gun fell out of his hand and Flynn pounced on it. Gordon made another move toward him to get the gun.

"Not so fast, genius. We're doing this *my* way now," Flynn said.

Coleman directed Banks to run back to his car and get something to secure the prisoners with. After he finished talking, he grew faint and closed his eyes.

"Stay with me, Mr. Coleman," Flynn said. "Talk to me. Don't pass out."

Banks returned with some rope and zip ties. In a matter of moments, they secured Gordon and Jones and shoved them into Coleman's car.

Flynn hustled back toward Coleman, who was lying flat on his back and moaning in pain. "We're going to get you some help, Mr. Coleman. Just hang in there," Flynn said.

Coleman turned his head and looked at Flynn.

"Tell Edith I love her," Coleman said. "And tell her that I'm sorry."

# CHAPTER 46

FLYNN TOOK A SEAT on the front row of the FBI press conference the following day a few minutes before noon. He wanted to hear Thurston describe Banks' heroics and all the sordid details to the public. It was the story his editor, Theresa Thompson, had been waiting on since the news first broke that someone had leapt out of an airliner with a million dollars and disappeared. Unless the President died, there wouldn't be a bigger story during the next 24-hour news cycle.

Banks slid into the seat next to Flynn. Her eyes sparkled beneath the glow of the television lights surrounding the room. "How are ya?" she asked.

Flynn took a deep breath. "Grateful to be alive after yesterday."

"Did you tell your editor what happened?"

He nodded.

"And she didn't give you the day off?"

Flynn smiled. "She offered but I declined. I wanted to see you up there getting the praise you deserve for what you did last night."

"You should be up there with me."

"I'm just a consultant, remember? Besides, I still have

a job to do."

"Well, I think you're going to be surprised. Thurston has something special planned."

Flynn watched Banks hustle away, ducking low to stay out of the view of the cameras. Less than a minute later, she reentered the room, following Thurston and several other FBI officials.

Thurston stepped forward and delivered a statement.

"As you might guess, the FBI has countless people who have worked tirelessly on apprehending the man responsible for not one, but two federal heists. The first one resulted in the theft of one million dollars, the second less than a week later for two hundred thousand dollars. But last night, those efforts paid off when FBI Agent Jennifer Banks arrested a suspect in the robbery, the man we believe to be behind the two heists.

"Unfortunately, she also had to arrest another man in connection with the case. Her former partner, Chase Jones. We are still sorting through the extent of Jones' involvement in the case, which will be revealed more in depth at a later time.

"For now, we believe that we have both men in custody who were behind the brazen attempts to steal federal money and abscond with it.

"However, it must be noted that Banks couldn't have done this without the help of a former FBI agent whose involvement in this case was vital. And that person is none other than former FBI Agent Harold Coleman."

Thurston turned to his left, his arm outstretched. The door swung open and an FBI official wheeled Coleman into the room.

Coleman smiled and waved with his left hand. His right arm was bandaged tightly, and a few nicks and scrapes on his face from the fray the night before remained visible. A lightning storm of flash bulbs lit up the room.

A grin flickered across Thurston's face. "At this time, I'd like to open the room up for questions regarding this case."

For the next hour, Thurston answered what questions he could, while deflecting other questions toward Banks and Coleman. They managed to keep quiet the details of what really happened the previous night. Speaking in vague generalities was enough to assuage a media corps hungry to let the world know that a man portraying himself as the second coming of D.B. Cooper was vanquished.

\*\*\*

AFTER THE PRESS CONFERENCE, Flynn slipped up next to the FBI official pushing Coleman down the hall.

"Mind if I take over?" Flynn said, flashing his credentials.

"Be my guest," the man said, giving way to Flynn.

Coleman cranked his neck at the sound of the familiar voice. He then looked straight ahead and sighed. "Mr. Flynn, to what do I owe this honor?"

Flynn laughed. "No, sir, Agent Coleman. The honor is all mine."

"So all it took for me to gain your respect was dragging these old bones to the middle of nowhere and waving a gun around?"

"You had my respect a long time ago—I just wasn't sure I believed you." Flynn paused. "But I most definitely do now."

"I hope you never know what it's like to go through life living under a cloud of suspicion and doubt," Coleman said as he shook his head. "I can deal with criticism, but I have a hard time with mistrust. And ultimately, that's what led to my demise within the Bureau. Nobody believed me—even when I knew I was right."

Flynn guided Coleman's wheelchair to the right. "I can't imagine."

"No, you can't. It's a living hell that someone has to experience in order to understand."

"But I do get being maligned and dismissed."

Coleman nodded knowingly. "Your time in the CIA?"

"Yeah. I saw terrible things done in the name of this country on supposed missions of peace—that were anything but peaceable."

"At least you got out with your dignity intact."

Flynn grunted. "Some people would question that assertion—I'm in journalism now."

"Good point."

"However, journalism does present some unique opportunities."

"Such as?"

"Such as a platform for you to tell your story—the whole thing."

Coleman shook his head. "I don't know if I want to do that. It might be too painful."

"Whoever said healing is pain free?"

Coleman sighed. "Okay. I'll do it. I'll tell you everything—just don't leave anything out, okay?"

"I'll tell it in your words, like a first-person article. Harold Coleman as told to James Flynn. Fair enough?"

"I'd be game for that."

"Excellent. However, I do have one question right now for you—not for print, of course."

"Fire away."

"So, do you really think the original D.B. Cooper is dead? Or was that your defense mechanism against all the criticism?"

Coleman took a deep breath as Flynn stopped outside an elevator and pushed the button. He shrugged. "Maybe. I don't know. At the time, the facts seemed to align that he didn't make it out alive. I mean, what criminal steals two hundred thousand dollars and vanishes. He didn't spend a dime of it—at least, not that we were able to track."

"And what about the money you found on the Tena Bar in 1980?"

"A distraction, perhaps? I don't know. That never made sense to me—and that money remains one of the biggest mysteries surrounding the case since we never recovered any of the other bills."

"So because the money never appeared in circulation, you're sure he died?"

"Sure as I can be. I mean, who steals all that money and never spends any of it?"

"Carlton Gordon."

"He's a megalomaniac, for sure. And that's the only reason why he never spent any of it. He wanted to be worshiped and adored like D.B. Cooper so he salted CenturyLink Field with it. That guy was destined to fail before he started."

Flynn chuckled. "Well, have you got a few minutes?"

Coleman nodded.

"Good. I want you to come with me and Banks to deliver some good news to our friend, Carlton Gordon."

Several minutes later, Flynn stood behind Coleman and his wheelchair along with Banks.

"Would you like to break the news to him?" Banks asked.

Coleman shook his head. "Nah, that's your job. I just want to watch."

"Suit yourself," she said.

The guard buzzed them into the holding area and they approached Gordon.

"What are you all doing down here? Did you come to gloat?"

Coleman smiled. "We just wanted to make sure everything was going well for you."

"Piss off, Coleman," Gordon growled. "Go catch a real criminal, one who's still out there—unless you're still pedaling that story about Cooper being dead."

"I'm looking at a real criminal," Coleman said, eyeing Gordon closely. Coleman then wheeled himself closer to Gordon. "But Agent Banks here has some good news for you, perhaps even unexpected."

Gordon sat up straight. "Oh?"

"Yes," Banks said as she slid a manila folder across the table toward him. "You're not going to die." She paused. "Well, not any time soon. In fact, you're going to be plenty healthy and live a long life—behind bars."

Gordon's eyes widened as he opened the folder and stared at its contents.

"How can this be?" Gordon asked.

"Sometimes a test says you've got cancer. Sometimes, it is wrong. This is one of those times."

"You mean, I'm going to live?"

Banks nodded. "Behind bars, that is. You've just got a stomach ulcer, one sure to get worse with time in prison. But nothing more. You'll live."

Gordon slammed his fists onto the table. "How can this be? I was going to die!"

"And now you're not—at least, not a free man."

# CHAPTER 47

THE NEXT MORNING, Flynn knocked on Banks' door while he juggled the two cups of coffee. After a few moments, the door swung open and Banks greeted Flynn with a smile—and a hug. She took one of the cups out of his hand and brought it up to her nose.

"Grande soy latte, no whip cream?" she asked.

"I never forget a coffee order," he said.

"You've got my down, that's for sure." Banks ushered him inside and shut the door behind him. "So, what's this big excursion you want to take today?"

He settled into her couch and propped his feet up on the coffee table. "You ever just get a nagging feeling that you can't let go?"

She nodded. "Uh, huh."

"So, I think you know where we're going today, don't you?"

She nodded again.

He jumped to his feet. "Good. Let's get going."

Flynn begged to drive, complaining that his rental, a Mercedes sports coupe, had almost been wasted on this assignment. "It was even a free upgrade."

Banks playfully rolled her eyes. "If you insist."

Within a few minutes, they were roaring south down I-5.

After a few minutes of silence, Banks' spoke up. "So, what do you think you'd be doing if you never went into the CIA or journalism?"

Flynn shrugged. "I've never thought about it much. I always wanted to be a spy as long as I could remember. And I always liked writing, too. Everything I do now seems like what I was destined to do."

"You never wanted to be a professional athlete or a doctor or a fireman?"

Flynn shook his head. "I always wanted to help people, but in a behind-the-scenes sort of way."

"So, now you're on television?" she said as she laughed.

"An unintended consequence of entering journalism in the twenty-first century. I'd be writing in relative obscurity for a news magazine if this were thirty years ago."

"Yet, here you are writing books and doing interviews all over the place."

"It's tiresome for me, that's for sure." He paused for a moment, lost in thought as he looked out at the Cascade Mountains surrounding them. "What about you?"

"What about me?"

"What would you do if you weren't an FBI agent?"

"I'd teach kindergarten or first grade," she said without hesitating.

"You've thought about this extensively, haven't you?"

She nodded. "I love my job, but there are days—" her voice trailed off.

"There are days in every profession. The grass is always greener."

"But I couldn't imagine even the worst parents ruining my day like sometimes this job does."

"Maybe you'll get an undercover assignment one day and find out firsthand."

She laughed. "I have a feeling that you'd be doing this, too, if you could."

"Maybe, but I've got the best of both worlds right now. Consulting with you and writing for *The National*."

Flynn pushed the Mercedes hard, somehow avoiding a ticket as he exited the Interstate. For nearly an hour, they bumped along a two-lane road until he finally pulled off to the side.

"You think this is it?" she asked.

He nodded. "Sure as I've ever been. We've got a little bit of a hike ahead of us, but I know where it's at."

Flynn locked the car and he led Banks through uncharted—though familiar—terrain. Remnants of snow still remained on the ground in the shadows, but the sun had sufficiently burned off the white powder along most of the forest floor.

After thirty minutes, Banks piped up. "Are you sure this is the right way?"

He nodded. "Just keep going."

Twenty minutes later, Flynn walked up over a rise and stopped. Banks hustled up the hill and stood next to him.

"What is it?" she asked.

He pointed, speechless.

They both broke into a sprint toward the cabin.

"What happened?" Banks asked.

The cabin less than a hundred yards away in front of them was torched, blackened by a fire that was squelched yet still smoldering in some places.

They both sprinted toward it, trying to wrap their

minds around the scene before him.

"Mark Justice," Flynn said as he laughed. "What a name. Almost as good as Dan Cooper."

He walked up the charred steps of the cabin and into the living room. The roof remained in place, but porous. Everything else appeared to be stripped out. No beds, furniture, appliances. Nothing. Just the empty shell of a cabin—empty except for a table.

"Would you look at this?" Flynn said as he walked toward the only structure in the room that wasn't burnt.

"Oh, my," Banks said, rushing over toward him.

A carton of cigarettes sat on the table along with a note.

Flynn picked up the note and read it aloud. "I'm glad you caught the copycat. He'll never get it."

"He'll never get it?" Banks repeated.

Flynn shrugged. "He'll never get why Cooper did it? I don't know. It's mind boggling."

Banks stared at the note. "But why leave us this? Why risk us finding his DNA everywhere and figuring out who he is?"

"His DNA won't show up in any database," Flynn said. "He hijacked the plane, disappeared with the money, and he's not interested in making a name for himself. The perfect crime."

"One day he's going to slip up—if he doesn't die first," she said, her voice trailing off.

"Well, at least we know what he looks like now."

\*\*\*

FLYNN SAUNTERED UP TO the corner of 22nd and Capp Street in San Francisco a mere two days later. He wanted to get home, but he needed to make a stop—a costly one that he hoped his editor would excuse on his expense report.

Resting against the wall of the drug store, the old man blurted out, "You got a cigarette I can bum off of ya?"

Flynn smiled. "As a matter of fact, I do."

"Wait a minute," the old man said. "I know that voice."

"Yes, you do, Doc," Flynn said. "It's me. And I come bearing gifts."

"Gifts? What did I do to earn a gift?"

"You helped us catch a thief."

Doc broke into a deep laugh that devolved into a cough. "I did?" he finally muttered.

"Yeah, Mr. Money Bags—or Mr. Stallion Cologne. Take your pick, but either way he was our guy."

"Really?" Doc said. "I never would've guessed."

"Yep. He's going to be behind bars for quite a while now."

"You don't say?"

"I do—and as a matter of fact, I've got more than just a gift—I've got a carton of Raleigh cigarettes."

"Best damn cigarette ever made," Doc said as he held his hands out.

Flynn placed the carton in Doc's hands and patted him on the back. "We couldn't have done it without you."

Doc laughed. "You got a light? I can't let these go unsmoked any longer."

Flynn pulled out a lighter from his pocket and sparked a Zippo for his new friend. "For you, Doc, I've got whatever you need. Just say the word."

The cigarette sizzled for a moment and began to smoke. Flynn patted Doc on the back.

Doc smiled. "They never think of everything," he said as he took a long drag.

## THE END

## About the Author

**R.J. PATTERSON** is a national award-winning journalist and award-winning author living in the Pacific Northwest. He first began his illustrious writing career as a sports journalist, recording his exploits on the soccer fields in England as a young boy. Then when his father told him that people would pay him to watch sports if he would write about what he saw, he went all in. He landed his first writing job at age 15 as a sports writer for a daily newspaper in Orangeburg, S.C. He later earned a degree in newspaper journalism from the University of Georgia, where he took a job covering high school sports for the award-winning *Athens Banner-Herald* and *Daily News*.

He later became the sports editor of *The Valdosta Daily Times* before working in the magazine world as an editor and freelance journalist. He has won numerous writing awards, including a national award for his investigative reporting on a sordid tale surrounding an NCAA investigation over the University of Georgia football program.

R.J. enjoys the great outdoors of the Northwest while living there with his wife and four children. He still follows sports closely.

He also loves connecting with readers and would love to hear from you. To stay updated about future projects, connect with him over Facebook or on the Internet at www.RJPbooks.com.

# Others Books in the James Flynn Series